Also by Michael Morpurgo

Arthur: High King of Britain
Escape from Shangri-La
Friend or Foe
The Ghost of Grania O'Malley
Kensuke's Kingdom
King of the Cloud Forests
Little Foxes
Long Way Home
Mr Nobody's Eyes
My Friend Walter
The Nine Lives of Montezuma
The Sandman and the Turtles
The Sleeping Sword
Twist of Gold
Waiting for Anya
War Horse
The White Horse of Zennor
Why the Whales Came
The Wreck of Zanzibar

For Younger Readers

The Best Christmas Present in the World
Conker
Mairi's Mermaid
The Marble Crusher

The War of Jenkins' Ear

MICHAEL MORPURGO

EGMONT

For Frances

EGMONT
We bring stories to life

First published in Great Britain in 1993 by William Heinemann Ltd
This edition published 2007 by Egmont UK Limited
239 Kensington High Street, London W8 6SA

Text Copyright © 1993 Michael Morpurgo
Cover illustration copyright © 2007 Oliver Burston

The moral rights of the author and cover illustrator have been asserted

ISBN 978 1 4052 2672 1

5 7 9 10 8 6

A CIP catalogue record for this title is available from the British Library

Printed and bound in Great Britain by the CPI Group

CHAPTER 1

'*BENEDICAT NOBIS OMNIPOTENS DEUS . . .*' THE FIRST grace of a new term. Henry Stagg, Headmaster and lord of all he surveyed, intoned with fresh vigour, his fingers flexing ominously as he gripped the back of his chair at High Table. Standing behind his bench at the window Toby Jenkins dared to lift his eyes. Mr Stagg looked thinner than he remembered, his neck longer somehow, more scraggy. But the voice was the same, sonorous and terrifying – 'Rudolph' they called him, when they were quite sure he couldn't hear them. Beside Rudolph, stiff in her grey-green suit with a butterfly brooch, stood Mrs Stagg, a head taller with straight dark hair and blood-red lips. Prunella he called her – 'Cruella' to the boys. Toby caught her eye and looked away quickly. The dying daddy-longlegs were still sidling clumsily along the window-ledge, clambering over each other in a vain effort to find a way out. There's no escape, thought Toby, not for you, not for me. Thirteen weeks and five days – ninety-six days until the Christmas holidays. There was half term, four days beginning November the sixth, but that was seven long weeks away.

Toby closed his eyes and swallowed back the dread that rose in the back of his throat, the dread he'd been living with since first he woke that morning. It had been with him during the silent ride with his mother on the Underground, and as they walked up the steps and into Victoria Station. He recalled how his stomach had heaved at the first sight of a green, red and white cap. His last hope of reprieve was shattered. There could be no doubt about it now. This *was* the day term began. They hadn't come too early. There had been no mistake. He was not Toby any more. He was Jenkins now, or 'Jinks'. Someone said what they always said. 'Hello, Jinks. Had a good hols?' Toby nodded. He didn't trust himself to speak. His mother went with him as far as the door of the carriage. She knew he hated her to wait. 'I'll be off then, Toby. God bless.' And she hugged him quickly and went away without looking back, leaving him with just the smell of her.

He knew by now there was no point in trying to stop the tears. They would come anyway in spite of himself. If he tried very hard though he could hold them in his eyes, just so long as he didn't blink.

He sat in the corner seat, his face against the windowpane as the carriage filled with the jovial banter of Redlands boys all bursting with news of their holidays. There were all the new jokes and all the old jokes. 'Have you heard this one? "Why did the submarine blush? Because it saw Queen Mary's bottom." ' In the joy of their reunion they hardly noticed Toby and that was a relief for him. Sooner or later of course they would, but by then he'd be ready for them. Simpson was the one to watch. He knew how to niggle better than most. When the train pulled out at last Toby went to the toilet where he locked himself in so that the tears could flow freely, so that he could steel himself, put away the last of Toby and become Jenkins.

The carriage was unnaturally quiet when he got back. 'And this,' said Simpson, 'is Jinks. He's been blubbing. He always blubs at the beginning of term. Say hello, Jinks.'

Until then Toby hadn't noticed him. There was a boy sitting in his seat by the window, a boy he had never seen before. His hair was longer than you were allowed at Redlands. 'He's a new bug,' said Simpson. The new boy moved up a bit so that Toby could sit down beside him. 'He's called Christopher,' Simpson went on.

'Christopher what?' Toby asked.

'Simon Christopher,' said the new boy quietly and he turned away to look out of the window.

* * *

'*Per Jesum Christum dominum nostrum. Amen.*' Shepherd's pie, cabbage, and after that it would be rice-pudding. Toby liked rice-pudding, especially the skin. The first supper was always the same. Toby sat in the babble of the dining-hall and looked down at his shepherd's pie. The others were eating already. He could not. The daddy-longlegs were trying to dance their way up to the top of the window. There were lots of them this year. 'Always the same in a dry summer,' his mother had told him. She'd be home from the station by now. They'd all be home, except him. Little Charley (no one called her Charlotte) would be shuffling around on her bottom, finger up her nose. His father would be back from the office (Toby never really knew what he did at the office). He'd be clipping the lawn edges, therapeutic he said; and Gran, trembling with Parkinson's disease in her wheel-chair, would still be doing the *Telegraph* crossword.

Toby ate the first mouthful of the first course of the first meal and swallowed without tasting. He'd had no breakfast, picked at his lunch, but he still had to force it down. You couldn't leave anything at Redlands, only as much as you could hide under your knife. Mr Birley called out from the end of his table.

'Jenkins,' he said, holding up the water jug.

'Sir?'

'It's empty.'

'Yes, sir.'

Mr Birley liked him. Mr Birley had always liked him because he sang in the choir and Mr Birley liked everyone who sang in the choir. There was a care-worn, hang-dog look about him but at least he was kind, and there weren't many like that. 'You do remember where it is?' He smiled as he handed him the jug and then the bread-basket. 'And you might as well get some more bread while you're at it.'

The dining-hall door closed behind him and he dawdled his way down the tiled passage towards the kitchen. He was alone again for the first time since the toilet on the train and he wanted to make it last as long as he could. He spent some time waiting outside the kitchen door picking the crumbs out of the bread-basket. Then he put his back against the swing-doors and pushed.

Mrs Woolland was at the sink, and there was a girl with her back to him slicing the bread. Mrs Woolland shook the suds off her arms and reached for a towel.

'Hello, Toby, back again then,' she said. At school hardly anyone else ever called him Toby. 'I'll take that.' She took the jug and ran the tap. 'You can help yourself to the bread.'

The bread was always kept in a deep wicker hamper in the corner of the kitchen, great towers of cut loaves, and the tallest towers were always the freshest. The girl was watching him now. He could feel it in the back of his neck.

'You remember Wanda, don't you?' said Mrs

Woolland. Toby didn't. 'She used to come up here a lot when she was a little girl, before your time I expect. Fourteen she is now, just left school. She's giving me a hand from time to time, aren't you pet?'

'Yes, Mum,' said Wanda. She blew her hair out of her eyes and threw her head back as she sawed at the bread. She came towards Toby holding a cut loaf like a concertina between her hands. She laid it in his basket and smiled at him.

'I've told you, I'm Mrs Woolland when I'm up at the big house, remember?'

'Yes, Mrs Woolland,' Wanda sighed confidentially at Toby and helped him squeeze the last slice of bread into the basket. Her eyes held his for a moment, and Toby found he could not look away.

'Don't forget the water,' said Mrs Woolland, bringing the jug over to him. The rice-puddings were laid out on the kitchen range waiting, the skins shiny-brown like rolling fields of toffee. 'Go on then, off with you,' she said. 'And don't drop it.'

Toby didn't drop it and he only slopped the water once as he turned the corner outside the music-room. He inched his way along the corridor, the din from the dining-hall louder all the time, but now he wasn't thinking about home or about how miserable he was. He was thinking about Wanda's eyes and wondered if they really could be green.

The rice-pudding was as good as it looked – it always was. Toby searched for a morsel of skin in his helping, his favourite bit, but found none.

'You like skin?' said a voice from across the table. It was the new boy, Christopher. How he knew that Toby liked the skin Toby could not make out. 'You can have mine then,' said Christopher. 'I can't stand skin.' He stood up, leaned across the table and scooped the skin on to Toby's plate – not at all the sort of thing you were supposed to do at Redlands. Toby looked down the table. It was all right. Mr Birley hadn't noticed. Toby was savouring his first mouthful of rice-pudding skin when the gong sounded behind him from the High Table. The dining-hall fell silent at once. Rudolph rose to his feet slowly, pushing himself up on his knuckles.

'That new boy on the window table,' he said, his eyes narrowing. 'Christopher, isn't it? Stand up will you. On the bench. And Jenkins, you too.'

Toby knew at once what it would be about, but he could see that Christopher was completely bewildered. Toby could feel his heart pounding in his ears as he stepped on to the bench and faced Mr Stagg. He'd only been back at school an hour or two and he was already in the middle of a nightmare.

'I don't know,' Rudolph began, his voice full of acid menace. 'I don't know what sort of a home you have come from, what sort of a school you have come from;

but here at Redlands we do not lean across the table, we eat what is put in front of us and we do not turn our noses up at Mrs Woolland's excellent rice-pudding. "Manners maketh man" is the motto of one of our great schools, and at Redlands we set great store by our manners, Christopher. Now, as this is your first meal with us I am prepared to turn a blind eye, but just this once. If ever I see you . . .'

'I don't eat the skin, sir.' Christopher spoke quietly. It was very matter of fact. There was no defiance in his tone.

'I beg your pardon,' said Rudolph, his brow twitching with irritation.

'I like the rest of it, sir,' Christopher explained coolly, 'but I don't eat the skin. I never do.'

'Do you not?' Rudolph said smiling thinly. 'Well, I'm afraid, Christopher, we will have to teach you an early lesson and it is this. Here you will do what you are told to do, not what you feel like doing. Food at Redlands is always eaten whether you like it or not and without complaint. We do not waste our food at Redlands, do you hear me?'

'Yes, sir, I know, sir. It was the same at my last school. That's why I gave it to him, sir, so it wouldn't be wasted.'

No one in the dining-hall could believe what they were witnessing. It was quite unthinkable for a boy to argue the toss with Rudolph. With Rudolph there was safety only in silent, abject acceptance. Rudolph roused was a very dangerous animal and every boy in the school knew it. The staff at the ends of their tables sat amazed but secretly delighted at this unexpected challenge. Not one of them would have dared face down Rudolph in public, nor in private, come to that. It was more than their jobs were worth. They waited with darting eyes for the massacre of the innocent. It didn't come.

'You will both sit down again,' Rudolph cleared his throat. 'Jenkins, you will return the rice-pudding skin to Christopher's bowl, and Christopher you will finish the entire contents of your bowl, skin and all. Mr Birley, you will please ensure that Christopher's bowl is clean. The window table will not leave the dining-hall until Christopher has eaten every bit of his rice-pudding skin. Is that quite clear?'

Toby sat down and passed his bowl over to Christopher. Christopher's face wore no expression as he spooned up the rice-pudding skin and laid it on top of his pudding. 'You may talk now,' said Rudolph as he sat down, and the dining-hall buzzed with muted astonishment. Spoons clinked on dishes again and the teachers rolled up their napkins and coughed away their embarrassment. On the High Table Rudolph sat brooding darkly, his fingers drumming on the arm of his chair. Toby finished what was left of his rice-pudding and scraped his bowl clean. Christopher too was eating his way through his pudding, but as everyone could see – and almost everyone was looking – he was eating his way around the skin and under it. By the time the gong sounded for grace the rice-pudding skin was still there, stiff and cold at the bottom of his bowl. When everyone else had left the room the window table stayed behind and sat in silence.

Mr Birley sneezed and blew his nose noisily. 'Well, Christopher,' he said sniffing. 'I think you'd better eat it otherwise we're going to be here all night. I have work to do and these boys would like to unpack. Matron – maybe you haven't met Matron yet – Matron will get very ratty indeed if they're not upstairs soon, and then I'll get it in the neck. No one likes it in the neck from Matron.' The boys laughed. 'Come along now, there's a good fellow, eat up.'

'I'm sorry, sir,' said Christopher, 'but I don't eat skin. I never have. I can't. It makes me sick.'

Mr Birley sighed and put his hand to his forehead. 'Now look here, Christopher,' he said, 'this has gone quite far enough already. This really isn't the way to get on here at Redlands, you know. All you have to do is close your eyes and swallow it, and then we can all forget about it.'

Christopher looked around the table and then down at the skin in his bowl. He shook his head. 'No, I can't,' he said. 'I just can't.'

Toby knew then, they all knew, that Christopher meant what he said, that he was not going to eat the rice-pudding skin. They could be sitting there till the morning – he would not eat it. Even Simpson knew it and Simpson was not very bright – he just talked a lot.

'Why don't I eat it, sir?' said Simpson. 'No one'll know.'

'I will,' said Mr Birley. 'He has to eat it. That's all there is to it. There are some things in life we don't like to do that we have to do, like teaching small boys. We shall just have to sit here in silence until Christopher decides to eat his rice-pudding skin. I'm sorry, but Mr Stagg made himself quite clear.' He blew his nose again and examined the contents of his handkerchief.

It was some minutes later when Mrs Woolland put her head round the dining-hall door. 'Can I clear, Mr Birley?' she said. 'Some of us have got to get home tonight.'

Toby hoped Wanda would come in and help Mrs Woolland, but she didn't. Mrs Woolland did it all on her own, put away the sauces and salts and peppers, wiped the tables and piled up the trolley. On her way out she spoke her mind: 'There's nothing wrong with my rice-pudding and the skin's the best bit.' And then she went out wheeling away the squeaky trolley, the plates and mugs clattering down the corridor. Toby watched the pair of daddy-longlegs struggling feebly in a cobweb at the bottom of the window and felt sorry for them all over again.

An hour or more later, and the daddy-longlegs had long since given up the fight. The spider was moving in for the kill when Custer padded into the dining-hall. Custer was Matron's golden retriever. He browsed in amongst the tables hoovering, nose to the ground, tail flourishing. Wherever Custer was, Matron was never far behind.

'Mr Birley,' she called. 'Are you in there, Mr Birley?' And then she was striding in through the dining-hall door. 'Well really, Mr Birley,' she said, shaking her head. 'What do you think you're doing?' Mr Birley knew better than to interrupt. 'I mean, really. It's all too silly. The whole school's talking about nothing else except rice-pudding. All this fuss over a bit of skin.' She turned her gaze on Christopher. 'So you're the troublesome new boy, are you? Bit old to be new, aren't you?'

'I'm thirteen,' said Christopher.

'And you don't like rice-pudding skin?'

'No.'

'And you won't eat it?'

'No.'

'Well that's clear enough anyway. Mr Birley, these boys have trunks to unpack and I'm not going to do it for them. Somehow, some way, that bit of skin has to be got rid of. Do we agree on that?' Mr Birley raised his eyebrows and shrugged his shoulders. 'You will all of you close your eyes. You too Mr Birley.' Toby waited until everyone had closed their eyes and then closed his. He heard Matron's starched uniform rustling behind him. Her hand was on his shoulder and she was leaning over him. 'Not a peep now, Jenkins,' she said. 'What the eye doesn't see, the heart won't grieve over.' Quite where she went to after that Toby could not tell. He could hear Custer skidding across the polished floor and his tail thumping against a chair leg, somewhere up near the High Table he thought. Then Matron was clapping her hands. 'All right,' she said. They opened their eyes. She was standing by the High Table, Custer sitting at her feet licking his lips. Mr Birley was looking at Christopher's bowl. 'It's gone,' he said.

'Magic,' said Matron, wiping her hands. 'You see? It wasn't as bad as all that was it Christopher? And in future don't be so childish.' Christopher smiled.

Heavy footsteps outside the door heralded Rudolph. 'Well?' he said.

'All gone, Headmaster,' said Matron. Everyone knew they didn't get on. Nothing was ever said of course, but neither disguised it very effectively. Matron went on. 'I'd like these boys for unpacking now, if you don't mind, Headmaster.'

'Of course, Matron,' said Rudolph stiffly; and he went on, his hand clutching his lapel: 'and let this be a lesson to you, Christopher. Because you are a new-boy, and because it is the first night of a new term I shall take no further action this time. But mark my words, the next time it'll be the cane. Very well, you may go now.' Matron had already gone, Custer at her heels, still hopeful.

'I want those boys upstairs for unpacking in two minutes, Mr Birley,' she called from outside. 'Two minutes!'

Toby didn't see Christopher again until he was brushing his teeth in the bathroom later that evening. They were standing side by side facing the mirror and alone. By now the rice-pudding incident had eclipsed all other beginning-of-term excitements. Toby looked across at him in the mirror as he rinsed his mouth. Christopher did nothing in a hurry. Even when he spat in the basin his movements were measured, almost elegant. If he was enjoying his fame, he showed no signs of it. He stared back at himself for a moment and then dropped his toothbrush into his mug. His face was pale, paler even than his oversized cream pyjamas. He looks more dead than alive, Toby thought, more like a ghost. The ghost spoke.

'I'm sleeping next to you,' Christopher said.

'I know,' said Toby.

'Why do they call you Jinks?'

Toby shrugged his shoulders. 'I don't know. They

always have. Partly my name I suppose, and maybe I'm not very good luck or something.'

Neither of them spoke for a moment. 'Do you like it here?' Christopher said, turning to him.

' 's all right, I suppose.'

'That's not what you really think is it? Why don't you say what you really think?' Toby didn't quite know what to say. He wasn't expecting this directness. 'Well, I hate it,' said Christopher, zipping up his sponge bag. 'Do you snore?'

'I don't think so.'

'Good,' said Christopher as he hung his towel on his hook.

Toby asked the question he'd been longing to ask. 'What would you have done, you know, if Matron hadn't come in like she did, if Custer hadn't . . . Would you have eaten it, in the end I mean?'

'No,' said Christopher. 'Course not. He'd have given in. They always do in the end.'

The dormitory was known as 'The Pit'. Five steps down and you were in a huge vaulted room with bare floorboards and high mullioned windows like a church. There were twelve beds on each side, and a wooden locker in between each. No one wanted to be in The Pit. It was the closest to Rudolph's flat and therefore the most dangerous. Any noise after lights-out and he could pounce without warning. It was freezing cold too and the beds were the old type – metal frames with springs that sagged in the middle. It was like sleeping in a squeaking, spiky hammock. But Toby was happier than he'd ever been on the first night of any term. His mind flitted from Wanda to Christopher and back to Wanda again. All thoughts of home and Mum and Dad and Gran and little Charley were forgotten. Matron had put the lights out some time ago but no one was asleep. No one would be asleep for hours, not on the first night. Suppressed giggling and whispering filled the darkness. The tower bell sounded in the quad outside, eleven o'clock. Toby looked across at Christopher. He lay still under his blankets, hands under his head. 'You awake?' Toby whispered.

'Yes,' said Christopher.

'What school were you at before?'

'A day-school down the end of our road, St Peter's.' He was talking louder than he should.

'You haven't been to a boarding school then, like this?'

'No, and I won't be staying for long either.'

The door opened suddenly. 'Talking! Who was talking?' Rudolph stood silhouetted in the doorway. The lights went on. 'Who was talking then? Come on. I heard you.' Everyone lay doggo and looked at everyone else.

'I was,' said Christopher propping himself up on his elbows. Rudolph hesitated for a moment, clearly surprised.

'You again. We really haven't made a very good start have we? Out of bed. Over here.' Christopher stepped into his slippers and put on his dressing-gown. He took his time. As he walked over to Rudolph everyone in the dormitory knew what would happen, everyone except Christopher, it seemed, for he showed no sign of fear, even in his voice.

'Yes, sir?' he said, looking Rudolph straight in the eye.

'Take off your slipper,' said Rudolph stonily.

'Which one, sir?' Christopher asked.

'Either.'

Christopher bent down and took off his right slipper. Rudolph almost snatched it out of his hand. 'There is no talking after lights-out. It is a rule. Do you understand about rules? I don't suppose they had rules in your Council school?'

'Yes, sir, they did.'

'There's things you are going to have to learn, Christopher, like not answering back for instance. Hold out your hand.' Rudolph gripped the heel of the slipper and struck three times. Christopher stood silent, his hand still held out in front of him. 'You want more?' said Rudolph, breathing hard.

'No, sir.'

'Get back to bed.'

Christopher walked slowly back towards his bed

undoing his dressing-gown cord. He lay down in bed, pulled the sheets up under his chin, and stared up at the ceiling. The lights went out and no one said a word until they could no longer hear Rudolph's footsteps, until the door of his flat shut behind him.

'You all right?' said Toby. But there was no reply.

When Toby woke next morning the bed next to him was empty. There was an excited huddle around Simpson's bed at the other end of the dormitory. Toby went over. Simpson was sitting cross-legged on his pillow and holding court.

'What's happened?' said Toby.

'Your friend,' said Simpson. 'He's run off.'

'You don't know,' Toby said.

'Oh, don't I? I only saw him go, that's all,' Simpson retorted. 'I was coming out of the bog early this morning, and there he was fully dressed. He walks right past me with his suitcase. Never says a word. Never even looks at me. Just walks down the stairs and out of the front door. I saw him from the bathroom window. He stops at the school gates, puts his suitcase down, takes off his shoes, shakes them, puts them on again and that was it. I'm telling you, he's gone, he's done a bunk.'

CHAPTER 2

MAJOR BAGLEY TAUGHT LATIN. HE WAS HARMLESS enough, unless you caught him in a bad moment and then he could be quite unpredictable. The trouble was that he drank too much. Everyone knew it, and indeed he made little attempt to hide it. Latin lessons that ended at break always finished with the same flourish. He would close his battered Latin grammar book – *Kennedy's Latin Primer* – take his watch out of his waistcoat pocket, flick it open with his finger-nail and announce: 'Time for my tipple and time for your milk.'

Milk, like everything at Redlands, was administered with military efficiency. Miss Whitland, the thin-lipped Assistant Matron, stood stiff and unsmiling, arms crossed above her blue canvas belt. Her job was to make sure that every boy drank his bottle of milk. You filed by under the archway, picked up your bottle, a straw through the silver top, and drank it leaning up against the archway wall. It was always cold, even in summer, and Toby drank it fast to get it over with. He didn't like cold milk because, like ice cream, it gave him a headache. Miss Whitland knew Toby of old and kept her eye on him making sure the bottle was empty before he returned it to the crate and threw his straw in the bin. Only after you had drunk your milk were you free for break. There often wasn't time in morning-break to go down to the park, and anyway that first morning of term no one would have wanted to. There was too much to talk about. Christopher's escape. Christopher and the slippering of the night before. Christopher and the rice-pudding incident. Rudolph glowering in morning assembly. The boys gathered in little groups in the quad and talked of little else.

Toby found himself subjected to a barrage of questions. Surrounded by a crowd of straw-sucking boys he told them all he knew about Christopher, and that wasn't much. It seemed that Simpson had put it about that he was bosom friends with Christopher. It wasn't true of course, he'd only spoken to him a few times. He told them that, but they didn't want to believe him. 'Did you see him go?' 'Did you try to stop him?' 'What was he like?' Unused to all this attention and uncomfortable with it, Toby made himself scarce at the first opportunity.

He was walking past the kitchen door, past the line of dustbins, when Wanda came out shrugging her coat over her apron. 'Here,' she called, and she beckoned him over. Toby hesitated, looking around him to be sure it was him she was calling. It had to be him, there was no one else about. She was taller than he thought and even more beautiful. Her hair was a sunburst of curls around her face. Toby found it difficult not to stare at her. He had to force himself to look down at her hands. She bit her nails, but then so did Toby. It only made him like her more. 'Here, aren't you the one in the kitchen yesterday?' Toby nodded. 'You heard about that boy have you? You ask me,' she went on, 'you ask me, I'd run away and all, like he did. What are you all doing here anyway? Don't your mum want you home? Don't she love you?'

'Course she does.'

'Then what are you doing here?'

It was the talk of home and his mother that choked Toby's voice. He turned away to hide it, but it was too late. She came after him. 'I'm sorry. I didn't mean nothing. Here.' She took him by the shoulder and turned him round to face her. She was holding out a bar of chocolate. 'Go on,' she said, and then conspiratorially: 'I filched it. Cooking chocolate from the kitchen. Good though.'

'Thanks,' said Toby, and when he took it their hands touched for just a moment.

'See you,' she said and she was gone, running off up the drive, her coat flapping behind her.

'Who's that?' Toby turned. It was Hunter. Hunter was king of the castle at Redlands, Captain of School and Captain of just about everything else too. He played every sport there was and played them better than anyone else. He always went home at the end of each term with armfuls of cups and prizes. He threw a javelin further than anyone else of his age in the country. He was national champion. Tall, lithe, a crown of close-cropped dark hair, he looked like a Greek warrior out of the history books.

Toby admired him only from a distance and was flattered whenever he spoke to him, which wasn't often. Hunter was flanked now by Porter and Runcy, both prefects and both sporting heroes, but Toby had never much liked either of them. They could be vindictive. It was best to steer clear.

'That girl,' said Porter, 'who was she?'

Toby was reluctant to tell them anything but he knew he had to. 'She works in the kitchen,' said Toby. 'Mrs Woolland's daughter.'

'An oik then is she? You got your eye on her have you?' Porter smiled his sideways smile.

Toby denied it hotly and began to walk away before they could ask any more questions.

'Jinks.' Hunter never lifted his voice – he never

needed to. Toby stopped and faced them again. 'What's her name?' said Hunter.

'Wanda, I think.' Toby tried to sound casual. Hunter came over to him and looked down at him from the clouds.

'You're on my side this afternoon, scrum-half. You any good?'

'Think so,' said Toby. 'I was in the Second Fifteen last year.'

'We'll see,' said Hunter. Toby watched him as he walked away, hands deep in his pockets. (Only prefects were allowed hands in their pockets.) The idea of having to tackle someone that big was not at all appealing. He was just glad that, this afternoon at least, Hunter would be on his side.

Toby liked rugby. At school there was little he really liked, just singing in the choir and rugby. That was all he was good at. He'd found out, almost by accident, that if you were small and you wriggled and side-stepped and jinked you could run past, run through or round much bigger boys; and there was no feeling in the world he liked better than to dive over the line to touch the ball down for a try. After he'd scored a try he could face even Mr Cramer for a double-maths period and not worry about it. Every try you scored meant you were instantly popular, temporarily maybe, but temporarily was better than not at all.

That afternoon, on a hard pitch freshly mowed, freshly marked out, Toby slipped in for two tries from the base of the scrum. He tackled ferociously and threw Hunter long and accurate passes. He grazed his knee in the process and had his knuckles hacked by Runcy, deliberately he thought. But as he trotted back across the gravel drive from the playing-fields in his new boots, Hunter came up alongside him.

'You were all right,' he said. 'You go on like that and you could make the First Fifteen.' Toby glowed inside. He knew that there was little enough hope of that. Hetherington was faster than he was and tougher. He was off-games at the moment. He'd been in the team the year before and he was bound to be first choice again for scrum-half. Still, Toby could hope. He knew how pleased his father would be if he could get in the first team, even get his colours. He wanted so very much to make his father proud of him, but he rarely managed it. Maybe if he could get into the First Fifteen and even get his rugby colours. He could dream.

He was still dreaming when he heard the sound of a car slowing outside the school gates and turning in on to the gravel. Mr Price – Pricey, the referee and rugby coach, pink-kneed in his long white shorts, shouted to everyone to stand back. A large black car came crunching slowly down the drive, past the rhododendrons. Everyone strained to see who it was. Toby heard before he could see for himself. 'It's that new boy,' said Hunter.

The car came to a stop outside the front door and Christopher got out pulling his suitcase behind him and shut the door. His mother – Toby imagined she must be his mother – was being greeted by Rudolph and Cruella at the front door. She beckoned Christopher towards her, but Christopher was looking at the crowd of boys now gathered on the edge of the playing-field. 'Simon!' Toby could hear the anger in his mother's voice. Christopher's eyes lingered on the boys for a moment or two. Toby felt a flicker of recognition and half lifted his hand in welcome, in sympathy. Christopher didn't seem to notice that. He walked around the front of the car and followed his mother indoors, Cruella leading the way.

'Right,' said Pricey, slapping the rugby ball. 'Enough gawping. Bath, and hang your kit up, properly mind.' He could turn his Welsh accent on like a tap.

The car stayed parked outside the front door all that afternoon. There was only one way Toby was going to find out what was going on and he was determined to try. His classroom opened into the oak-panelled hall that was the heart of the school. It served variously as an assembly hall every morning, a cinema on Sunday evenings, and a library. The wide steps that led from the hall were known as the Bloody Steps. Carpeted in deep crimson, with polished brass stair rods, they led to Rudolph's apartment, Rudolph's study. To be summoned up those dreaded steps meant only one thing – the cane. Everyone knew that if you stood at the bottom of the Bloody Steps, by the bookcases, and pretended to be looking for a book, you could often hear what was going on inside the study. But how was he going to manage to bluff his way into the hall in the first place? Mr Cramer may have looked doddery but he was wily, and you didn't get out of his maths class that easily. He wasn't going to be fooled by the usual lame excuses – they might prove effective with the younger, greener teachers, especially with the French mistress, Madame Lafayette who taught art too and who wore sandals and long flowery skirts. Either she believed anything she was told or she didn't mind half the class being absent at the same time. Mr Cramer wasn't like that. 'Can I go down, sir?' meant you needed a short trip to the lavatory and were expected back soon. 'Can I go down successful?' implied a need for a longer absence in the same place. Both had been tried already on Mr Cramer that lesson, and both had failed. Toby wasn't the only one who wanted to find out what was going on. Greater ingenuity was needed. It took Toby half an hour to think up his scheme. It had risks but it was worth it. He would try it. He put up his hand.

'Please, sir,' he coughed and sniffed as best he could. 'Please, sir, it's my hayfever.'

'I didn't know you had hayfever, Jenkins.'

'Only sometimes, sir. Matron says that if I feel it coming on I've got to take my tablets.' He hoped he didn't need to say any more. Matron was the key that opened most doors with most of the teachers. Just the mention of her name was often enough, and so it proved this time.

'Very well, Jenkins. Two minutes.'

Toby closed the classroom door behind him and found himself alone in the hall. He was quite confident that Mr Cramer wouldn't check his story with Matron. He could already hear voices from inside the study but could not make out what they were saying. He stole across the polished floor, unable to stop his sandals squeaking as he went. He peered round the corner. Christopher was sitting outside the study on the settle, motionless, his hands on his knees like the statue of an Egyptian pharaoh. The study door opened suddenly and Christopher's mother was coming out. Toby had just enough time to back out of sight along the bookcase. He felt the piano behind him, crouched down and crawled under, backwards. There was nowhere else to hide. 'One thing I'm sure of, Headmaster,' he heard Christopher's mother say, 'is that once he has made a promise he keeps it. He has promised me and he has promised you that he will never again try to run away. Isn't that right dear?'

'Yes, Mother.' Christopher's voice was quite calm.

'Don't you worry, he'll be all right now, won't you,

Christopher?' It was Cruella, but Christopher did not reply. Christopher's mother came down the steps. 'I'll see you at half term then,' she said without even a glance at Christopher.

Rudolph and Cruella, only feet away from Toby's hiding-place now, walked across the hall on either side of her and Christopher followed along behind them, his hands clasped behind his back. 'I'm sure we shall all get along splendidly,' Rudolph was saying. 'Redlands is a friendly sort of place. Everyone gets on here. He'll find that out soon enough.'

'I'm sure he will,' said Christopher's mother, and then they were out of sight, down the hallway towards the porch and the front door. Toby heard the front door open and was debating whether he should make a dash for the classroom now or wait until Rudolph and Cruella had gone back into the study. He never had the time to make up his mind.

He heard a cough from behind him. There were two sturdy legs in dark stockings and flat shoes and one of the feet was tapping. Only Matron wore shoes like the police. 'Jenkins,' she said. 'If I was a boy here that is probably exactly where I should spend as much time as I could, under the piano; but I am not a boy, I am Matron. Crawl out Jenkins, crawl out.' Toby stood up before he should have done and banged his head on the piano. The strings reverberated. Matron smiled at him.

'Well, that'll knock some sense into you, won't it?'

'Yes, Matron.' He was still rubbing his head and about to go back into the classroom when he heard Rudolph's voice from across the hall. 'Jenkins, what do you think you are doing out of class?' Christopher was there with him.

'He has a headache, Headmaster,' said Matron. 'I've given him something. It's better now, isn't it, Jenkins?' She turned her attention to Christopher. 'Back again then are we?' Christopher nodded. 'Staying this time are we?' Toby never quite knew when Matron was being serious and when she wasn't.

'Oh, he'll be staying, Matron,' said Rudolph, 'you can be quite sure of that. And I want no special treatment either. He's in your class, Jenkins. Take him along. Matron, may I have a word?' And the two boys were left alone in the hall.

'This school, it smells of cabbage and polish,' Christopher said sniffing. Toby had always noticed that too, particularly at the beginning of term.

'I'm glad you're back,' Toby said as they walked towards the classroom, and he meant it. He didn't know what else to say, but he thought he had to say something.

'I'm not,' Christopher said, and they went in together.

'Now there's a thing. You would have thought it a mathematical impossibility,' said Mr Cramer, peering at them over the rim of his glasses. 'One goes out, two come back.' He pointed to the empty desk beside Toby's. 'Your desk I believe, Christopher. Sit down.' Every eye in the room followed Christopher to his seat. 'We are doing long division. Have you ever done long division?'

'No, sir,' said Christopher, 'but I'll learn. I learn very quickly.'

To everyone's surprise – boys and staff alike – Christopher did learn very quickly. At his Council school he had never before done French or history or geography or Latin – a fact which amazed everyone at Redlands – but it seemed to make no difference whatsoever. Within a few days he appeared to have mastered what had taken Toby several long years of grinding learning. He could decline the first and second declensions in Latin and he already knew his way around at least a dozen French irregular verbs – all the tenses, even the subjunctive. He knew almost every capital on the globe, and had learnt by heart the names and dates of all the Plantagenet kings. He had, or so it seemed, a photographic memory. He could learn a poem on reading it and recite it without hesitation in class the next morning.

Yet in spite of all this brilliance, or perhaps because of it, Christopher had made no lasting friends or admirers except Toby. Brought up as they were to be wary of intelligent eccentrics, the boys kept their distance. Even the teachers were only grudgingly impressed. Toby overheard them once when he was waiting outside the staff-room door. Madame Lafayette was proclaiming enthusiastically that she had never had such a brilliant student, either in France or in England. 'It's just like as if 'e 'as the French blood in 'im,' she said. 'You say a word just once and 'e pronounces it like a French person. Mind you 'e can't paint for toffee.'

'Bright boy, maybe the brightest we've ever had, but surly,' said Major Bagley.

'If you ask me, he asks too many questions,' Mr Cramer said. 'Can't stand boys who ask too many questions.'

And that was the main problem. He unnerved everyone by asking too many penetrating and unexpected questions. Bare facts seemed unimportant to him, uninteresting. He always had to know the whys and wherefores. For instance, it wasn't enough for him just to know the date of the South Sea Bubble or the Treaty of Utrecht or the Bill of Rights or the War of Jenkins' Ear, he would go on questioning until either the teacher became irritated or until he was satisfied. As a result he would never write the regulation five lines on anything. His account of the Wars of the Roses covered two sides of paper and yet he seemed to do it in the same time it took Toby and the others to write their five lines. The teachers put it down to inexperience, to lack of early training at his Council school. He would catch up, in time.

But in divinity it was quite evident that he had no

catching up to do at all. The local vicar, the Reverend Jolyon – 'Holy Jo' the boys called him – came in every Friday and Tuesday morning to teach divinity. Always nervous and uneasy in front of the boys, they knew it and ragged him mercilessly, even calling him 'Holy Jo' to his face. In all the time Toby had known him he had never once lost his temper and Toby admired him for that. But now with Christopher in the class Holy Jo became a changed man, for it was soon clear to him and to everyone else that Christopher knew his Bible through and through. He knew all the parables and what's more he understood what they meant. He could quote the prophecies of Isaiah and many of the Proverbs. He knew Psalm 23 and the Sermon on the Mount by heart. Holy Jo grew visibly happier and more relaxed as each lesson demonstrated yet greater depths of Christopher's knowledge and understanding.

Toby was there when Holy Jo called Christopher to his desk after the lesson was over. 'Christopher,' he said, 'is your father a vicar by any chance?'

'No,' said Christopher. 'He's a carpenter, makes doors, windows and things.'

'Well I'm amazed,' said Holy Jo, shaking his head. 'Utterly amazed. We must talk more, we must talk more.'

Rugby was every afternoon, whatever the weather, except Sundays and Tuesdays. Tuesday was cross-country running. Christopher's trunk hadn't arrived until the second week of term and when he first turned out on the rugby pitch he looked very fragile in his shorts. Toby saw him wandering on to the pitch and he seemed to be in a world of his own. Pricey asked him if he'd ever played rugby before and he shook his head. 'I've played football,' he said. 'What do you have to do?' Everyone laughed at that.

'Well it's quite simple really,' said Pricey. 'You just pick up the ball and run with it. You run all the way down the pitch and you touch it down over the line. And anyone on the other side – you've got a blue shirt on, so that means the reds – anyone in a red shirt will try to tackle you and if you see anyone in a red shirt with the ball then you tackle him. We'll show him Hunter, shall we?' Hunter threw the ball to Porter, who tried half-heartedly to run past him. No one runs past Hunter. The tackle came in hard and low and Porter was lifted into the air before he crashed to the ground, the breath knocked out of him. 'See?' Pricey laughed. 'Like that.'

But Christopher seemed already to have lost interest.

Pricey put him on the right wing for that first game so he wouldn't get hurt and he had a quiet word with the reds to take it easy. 'Let him in gently,' he said, which of course was not at all what the reds had in mind.

Whenever Toby looked up from the base of his scrum Christopher was standing, hands behind his back, often facing the wrong way, often offside. Toby told him time and again that he had to keep behind the ball, but Christopher was not listening. He kept gazing up at the clouds, as if he was looking for a plane, Toby thought. Then Runcy sliced a kick and the ball bounced across the field and came to rest at Christopher's feet. He looked down at it as if it was some kind of intrusion. Pricey shouted at him. They all shouted. 'Pick it up! Pick it up!' Christopher bent down and picked up the ball in both hands. 'Run, run!' Toby shouted. He seemed not to know which way to run. 'That way!' Toby cried, haring across the pitch towards him and pointing to the goal posts. For a moment Christopher stood looking at the red shirts as they came at him. Then he started running slowly, tentatively, sideways across the field. They were screaming at him to pass it. If he heard them, he didn't appear to understand. Hunter was running alongside him. 'Here, here! Pass it!' And then Christopher stopped dead in his tracks and turned to face the pack of converging red shirts.

Toby expected, and everyone expected, that he would just throw the ball in the air or drop it. He did neither. Instead he tucked the ball under his arm and ran at them. He sliced his way through them, going like the wind for the corner flag. When the cover came across to tackle him he simply bounced off his outside foot and wrong-footed them all, including Porter who was left floundering by the touch-line. Christopher touched the ball down between the posts and stood wiping the mud off his hands. There was no whistle. Pricey was so stunned he had forgotten to blow it. The boys stood gaping and silent except for Toby who ran up and clapped him on the shoulder. He felt suddenly very proud of Christopher and very fond too. 'Well done!' he said, picking up the ball. He noticed that Christopher was hardly breathing. He'd just run fifty yards and he was hardly breathing.

In the communal bath afterwards Toby and Christopher sat side by side, chest deep in hot brown water, scrubbing the mud off their knees. The bath was the size of a small swimming-pool. From the other end Porter was glaring at them. 'Hey you! New bug!' The bath fell silent.

Christopher was splashing water over his face. 'Me?'

'Yes, you. I was watching you. You never tackled, not once. Anyone can run.'

'I suppose so,' said Christopher, stepping out of the bath and picking up his towel.

'Bit of a coward then, are you?' Porter had his blood up. Toby knew how it would end. He got out too and tried to lead Christopher away. But Christopher would not leave.

'No,' he said. 'It's not that. I just don't want to tackle, that's all. There's no point in hurting someone, not if you don't have to. Doesn't help.'

'Doesn't help what?' Porter was out of the bath now and advancing towards Christopher, flicking his towel at him.

'Leave him be,' said Toby, surprised at his sudden surge of courage, 'he hasn't done anything.'

Hunter tried to restrain Porter from behind but Porter shook him off. They were nose to nose now, Runcy egging Porter on. 'Fight! Fight!' The cry went up from all around the changing-rooms and the wash-room filled with boys, silent with eager anticipation. Christopher stood, his towel around his waist and looked back at Porter, unflinching.

'It's always the same with your kind,' Porter sneered. 'You're an oik, aren't you?' and he pushed Christopher in the chest. 'Come from an oik's school, didn't you?'

'Using force is a sign of weakness,' Christopher replied coolly. 'Think about it. Just because you knock someone down, doesn't make you right, does it? You can hit me if you like. Whatever you do I won't hit you back, so there really isn't any point in starting anything, is there?' And he walked away.

Porter blurted a few words of vicious invective, stabbing his finger at the departing Christopher. 'Next time, oik!' he bellowed. 'Just you wait. Next time!'

Toby followed Christopher out. 'Jesus,' Toby said, whistling through his teeth. 'You got lucky.'

Christopher stopped suddenly and turned on him.

'Please don't blaspheme,' he said quietly. 'And understand this, Toby, with me nothing is lucky, nothing is unlucky. Everything is meant.'

Each day at school was a ritual of meals and lessons and games and more lessons and more meals and prep and bed. Toby dreaded them all. But of all of them Tuesday was the day Toby dreaded most. And he wasn't alone. The Tuesday run was compulsory, like most things at Redlands, unless you were off-games. Matron's surgery was always unusually busy on Tuesday mornings. It took place rain or shine, snow, ice or fog. It was three miles up around the village running the gauntlet of the village boys, the 'oiks' as they called them, dodging their insults and sometimes their stones. It took you past the village school, past Mr Woolland's farm and back through the school park. You weren't allowed to stop, even on the hills – there was always a master about to ensure that. Anyone caught trying to take a shortcut had to repeat the whole run escorted by a master on a bike. But much as Toby hated the pain in his legs and the stitch in his stomach, this term he had something to look forward to, something to take his mind off it. There was always a chance that he might catch a glimpse of Wanda in her garden. If she was there she would wave to him and he would wave back. It was a moment worth any amount of suffering.

Sunday was the only day Toby really looked forward

to. There would be no lessons to survive and no prep he couldn't do. There was chapel in the morning, of course, but Toby sang in the choir and liked the hymns and the anthems and wearing a surplice. It made him feel good. In chapel you could think your own thoughts and be alone, even with everyone sitting around you. There was letter writing after that and then lunch – Sunday roast, with apple or rhubarb crumble afterwards, and custard with lots of brown sugar. But best of all was the long afternoon in the park below the school. The boys shared it with Mr Woolland's cows and sheep. There were rabbits and slow-worms and even the occasional roedeer. It was their paradise. There'd be blackberries to plunder, forests of oak and elm to explore, trees to climb and conkers to collect. In the evening there'd be a film in the hall, cartoons, *Tom and Jerry* or *Popeye*, followed by Charlie Chaplin or Buster Keaton. Then storytime with Matron or Miss Whitland in the dormitory and then sleep. The only trouble with Sundays was that they ended and they were followed by Mondays. But they came round again, so Toby always had something to look forward to.

Two Sundays into the term and Christopher had volunteered for the choir. Toby found himself sitting next to him in the choir-stalls, not by arrangement. They just liked being together, content if silent, in each other's company. Christopher seemed to know all the hymns and followed the service avidly in his prayer book. He prayed properly – with his eyes closed, Toby noticed – as if he was really praying. Toby envied him that. He could never finish a prayer without his mind wandering off long before the Amen.

Toby's letter home that Sunday was typical. You had to write one side at least neatly, and have it read by the master-on-duty, Pricey it was this Sunday. Toby wrote it in large handwriting, you covered the paper more quickly that way. He could never remember what he'd written the week before. His mother often said he told them the same news again and again.

'Dear Mum and Dad and Charley and Gran, I am well. How are you? I am in Four A this term and my desk is near the window. I am in The Pit and a new boy called Christopher is next to me. Matron says can I have cod-liver oil and malt again? So can I? And can you send me more name-tapes she says. And Mr Cramer says I must have extra maths again, so can I? I played rugby yesterday and scored a try. That's four in all I've scored this term so far. Hunter says that maybe I'll be in the First Fifteen. I hope so, but there's another boy and he's very good so I probably won't. I hope Gran is better and that there's no more greenfly on Dad's roses. I hope Charley's been good. I've eaten all my tuck-box biscuits so could you send me some more? Squashed fly are my best. I've got a new friend, he's called Christopher. He's the one that sleeps next to me in The Pit. Lots of love. Toby'

The letter passed Pricey's inspection and he was free. That afternoon found him showing Christopher the park. Dressed in regulation blue boilersuits and wellies he took Christopher through the spinney, down Woody Hill to the river that ran along the bottom of the park. From there you could look back and just see the chimneys and castellated walls of the school and the bell tower with the weather-vane stuck pointing North. Turn around and on the other side of the river, up across three fields and on the far side of a heart-shaped wood – Innocents' Copse they called it – there was the village. It was just a few houses, a pub, a church and a chapel.

'That's Ickham,' Toby said. 'You see the grey-roofed farmhouse below the church? That's Mrs Woolland's house and Wanda's.' He hadn't meant to mention her – it had just slipped out.

'Wanda?' said Christopher.

'You know, the girl in the kitchen.' He was as nonchalant as he could manage. 'Her father farms most of the land over there, and our park. They're his cows. We go beagling with him sometimes, in the winter, after hares. That's his hay-barn, just across the river.'

Later they found a slow-worm basking on a stone behind the swimming-pool hut. 'Runcy killed one last term,' Toby told him, 'bashed it over the head. Said he thought it was a baby adder, but he knew it wasn't. He just wanted to kill it, that's all.' Christopher crouched down, picked it up gently and let it curl around his wrist.

'We'll hide it then,' he said. They made sure no one was around and then released it into a bank of long grass and dusty nettles, and watched it disappear. A red admiral caught Toby's eye as it sunned itself on a bramblebush nearby.

'You like blackberries?' he said.

They picked from the long low bushes beyond Willow Copse. They weren't the best blackberries in the park, but Toby knew the best had already been picked clean. They were shrivelled with autumn and pippy but that mattered to neither of them. They gorged themselves until there was none left worth eating. Suddenly Christopher was coughing and laughing, his eyes watery. 'I swallowed a fly,' he gasped.

'I don't know why you swallowed a fly,' Toby quipped. 'Perhaps you'll die.' And he banged Christopher on the back until the coughing and spluttering subsided. They had had enough of blackberries.

They reached the rhododendron forest at the top of Woody Hill, and Toby decided to show him his camp, long since abandoned. Toby pulled aside the branches that had grown across the opening and crawled in.

'We make camps sometimes, in the summer mostly. There's lots of them like this. We have wars.'

'What for?' Christopher asked.

'Well, fun I suppose,' Toby said. Sometimes Christopher's questions made him feel uncomfortable. He never said what you expected him to say. Toby was standing in the middle of the camp now looking up at the canopy of rhododendron branches and leaves. It was so thick you could scarcely see the sky beyond.

'There's a nest up there,' Toby said pointing. 'Blackbird I think. See it?' Christopher didn't reply, and when Toby turned round he saw Christopher stagger and fall.

'God, dear God,' he cried, and fell forward on to his face, his arms outstretched in front of him. Toby ran to him and turned him over. Christopher was unconscious, his hair matted with earth, leaves clinging to his face. There was blood trickling from his nose. Toby brushed away the earth and leaves and shook him.

'Christopher? Wake up! Wake up!' Christopher lay still. Toby put his ear to his chest and then to his mouth. Christopher was not breathing.

CHAPTER 3

TOBY SLAPPED CHRISTOPHER'S FACE, TENTATIVELY at first, then harder and harder, rocking his head from side to side, but there was still no sign of life. He took him by the shoulders and shook him again. 'Come on Christopher, come on.' He could hear the panic in his voice and felt the scream rising inside him. A hollow gurgle in Christopher's throat gave him sudden hope, but in spite of all the shaking and shouting it came to nothing. A death rattle, Toby thought. Jesus, he's dead. He's really dead. He stood up and backed away, unable to take his eyes off Christopher's face. He was sobbing now, his hand in his hair pulling at it. 'Please God, no,' he cried. 'Please God.'

Blurred by tears, Christopher seemed to Toby to melt and then to move, his leg first and then his head. Toby wiped his eyes clear and saw that Christopher was on one elbow and trying to sit up. He watched him, still backing away, still not believing the evidence of his own eyes. Christopher was coughing and looking around him, blinking. 'Help me,' he whispered, holding out a hand. 'Help me up. Are you there, Toby?' Toby hesitated only because he could not get it out of his head that Christopher was dead, quite dead, he was sure of it. It flashed through his mind that this could be Christopher's ghost climbing out of his body. Christopher was squinting up at him. 'Is it you, Toby? I can't see you properly.' He was rubbing his eyes. Toby found his voice at last.

'I'm here,' he said. 'What happened?' And then he was by Christopher's side, helping him to his feet. Christopher steadied himself, his hands on Toby's shoulders.

'It's better now,' he said. 'I can see you better now.'

'I thought you were dead,' Toby said. 'Do you get fits?'

Christopher shook his head and took a deep breath. 'You must promise,' he said, 'you must promise me never to tell anyone about this. I can trust you can't I?'

'Course,' said Toby. He could feel Christopher's fingers digging into his shoulders.

'What I'm going to tell you,' Christopher went on slowly, 'I have never told a living soul.' Toby looked down to escape the intensity in Christopher's eyes. 'You must look at me,' said Christopher, shaking him, 'otherwise you will not believe me.' Toby made himself look up. 'I have visions, do you understand me? I see visions. This wasn't the first time, Toby. I've had them for years now. It's always the same, a blinding light and then he comes through it and stands as close to me as I am to you now, so close I could reach out and touch him.'

'Him?'

'Jesus,' said Christopher. 'It's Jesus, I know it is. He was there, right there, in the corner. I swear it. And he isn't at all as he is in the pictures. He's small and dark with eyes that go right through you.'

'But how do you know it's him?' Toby asked.

'Because he told me. He told me he was, and I believe him.'

'Well maybe it's just sort of a dream,' Toby said. 'Maybe you had a fit perhaps – I've seen them before. Runcy, you know, the prefect in our Dorm, he has fits – epileptic. I've seen him. You were just like him.' Christopher shook his head and sighed deeply.

'You still don't understand, do you? It's not a fit. It's a vision, but it isn't just a vision. He talks to me. Jesus talks to me. He's calling me.'

'What do you mean?'

'He tells me, tells me what I have to do. You don't believe me, do you?'

'I'm not really sure,' said Toby. He was, in fact, completely sure that Christopher must either be mad or sick, maybe both.

'He tells me that I am him reincarnated, come back. I am Jesus, and like he did before me I have to try to save the world. And today he told me that the time has come, that I have to start my work right away and with you at my side. You will be my Peter, my Rock, my first disciple.'

'Me?' said Toby. 'Why me?'

'Because I have chosen you, because my father has chosen you and because he knows I can trust you. Like the Jesus before me I will need friends, followers and disciples to help me spread the word. Will you follow me?'

Toby struggled for an answer that would not offend. He still thought the whole thing was preposterous, ridiculous; yet there was something unearthly in Christopher's cobalt blue eyes, something in the sincerity of his voice, that could not be denied.

'You don't believe in me do you?' Christopher turned away.

'Look,' said Toby, 'I want to believe you, but . . .'

'I know,' said Christopher nodding, 'I know, but a small miracle might help to persuade you. You need proof. Is that it?'

Toby hadn't even thought of it, but now that he did it made some sense. If Christopher could work miracles like Jesus, then he'd have to believe in him, no matter what.

'All right then,' Christopher went on. 'You'll have your miracle. But promise me this, when it happens, and it will happen, don't just put it down to luck or coincidence, because it won't be either.' And Christopher walked past him out of the camp.

'What're you going to do?' Toby called after him, but by the time he'd followed him out Christopher was already half way down Woody Hill, hands deep in his boilersuit pockets. 'You've got your hands in your pockets. Only prefects are allowed!' He did not reply and he didn't take his hands out of his pockets either.

For several days after that the two of them hardly spoke to each other. Toby's marks in class were even worse than usual, but now it was not out of laziness as it usually was. He just could not tear his mind away from the incident in the camp, from Christopher's claim to be the second Jesus, from Christopher's promise of a miracle. He would find himself forever looking at Christopher for some sign of godliness, some proof of anything that would help him make up his mind. There were no glowing halos or singing angels to help him. In choir practice he didn't look any more angelic than anyone else. All he saw was a silent, solitary boy who was almost always reading or studying; and still the promised miracle hadn't happened.

Even Toby's rugby went to pieces. Hetherington came back from the sick room and took Toby's place as scrum-half in the first team 'probables'. Toby was relegated to the 'possibles'. Nothing was going right. When the end of fortnight marks were given out in Mark Reading on Saturday morning Christopher was top in every subject. Toby was studying his face for any sign of vanity as Rudolph congratulated him. 'The highest mark in divinity ever recorded at Redlands! Excellent, quite excellent.' And beside him Holy Jo nodded and beamed his delight. On Christopher's face Toby saw not even a glimmer of pride. Toby himself was third from bottom of the class and was put 'on report' which meant that every lesson during the next fortnight had to be graded and he had to report to Rudolph at the end of each day to show his report card. He knew it would be the cane for him if he was ever given a black mark, and he knew from experience that whatever he did he could not now avoid a black mark – once you were 'on report' you never could. The clouds were gathering.

The team list for the first match of term went up on the board outside the staff room. Toby didn't even bother to look, he didn't want to have his own failure confirmed. He saw Porter and Runcy clapping Hetherington on the back and Pricey laughing with them. Toby turned away and made for the chapel. The chapel was the only place at Redlands where you could be miserable in peace. There were the lavatories, of course, but they smelt and people were always coming in and kicking open the doors. He sat where he always did when he came to the chapel on his own, under the stained-glass window where Christ was rising from his tomb and the helmeted Roman soldiers, big-toed in their sandals, were sleeping at his feet. The red sacristy light flickered on the altar. The chapel was dark. An owl hooted outside so close that it could have been inside, and then there was silence, blessed silence. Toby laid his head on his hands and wished he was dead. There would be no triumph now to report to his father, no rugby colours, only the same dreaded reports: 'Idle.' 'Toby could do better.' 'Inattentive.' 'A wasted term.' They echoed in his head and he found the back of his hands were wet with tears.

'Toby,' said a voice behind him, Christopher's voice. 'You wanted a miracle, remember. Well you won't have to wait long now.' Toby swivelled round. Christopher was standing at the chapel door. 'Tomorrow,' he said. 'It'll be tomorrow.' And he was gone.

Toby did not sleep much that night. Beside him Christopher slept as he always did, on his back, sheets pulled up neatly under his chin, his hands folded on his stomach. He hardly seemed to be breathing. All night Toby watched him, and by morning he had convinced himself that Christopher must be a fraud, that it was all too unlikely, too impossible to believe, that there would be no miracle, that he had to forget about Christopher's story, to dismiss it utterly from his mind.

He had just dropped off when he heard the bell. Miss Whitland breezed through The Pit. 'Rise and shine. Rise and shine.' And Toby wondered where the night had gone. As he brushed his teeth he could not help watching Christopher washing his face. Their eyes met in the mirror. 'I don't believe you,' Toby said quietly.

'I know you don't, but you will,' said Christopher as Simpson came yawning into the bathroom.

'What's up with you, Jinks?' he said, running the tap in the basin next to his.

'Nothing.'

'Your lady-love is it?'

'What?'

'Oh come on. That Wanda. Everyone knows you're stuck on her. You can't take your eyes off her can you? Porter told me.' The truth was that he hadn't given Wanda a second thought since the incident in the den, but he knew better than to deny it.

He shrugged. 'She's all right,' he said, and thankfully Simpson brushed his teeth, gargled and made no more of it.

By break time there was still no miracle. Toby had cheated his way through a French dictation. It was the only way he could do it. Fortunately Madame Lafayette always let them mark their own, so Toby awarded himself a believably moderate mark and no one seemed to question it. Perhaps, he thought, perhaps everyone else is doing the same thing anyway.

At break the straw in his milk closed itself and wouldn't suck properly so he took it out and drank straight from the bottle. The milk was so cold that morning that he didn't realise he had nicked his lip on the bottle. He was leaning up against the kitchen wall whittling a stick with his sheath-knife when he saw Wanda coming towards him wiping her hands on her apron. 'Hello stranger,' she said. 'Your lip's bleeding. You been in a fight?' Toby touched his mouth with the back of his hand and wondered how it had happened. He shook his head. 'Here, I'll do it,' said Wanda and she licked her handkerchief and dabbed his lip gently. 'Nothing much,' she said. She was very close to him. She smelt of pastry and there was flour on her cheek. 'Why so glum, Toby?' she said. 'Mum said you'd be cock-a-hoop. One of Mum's favourites you are. D'you know that?'

'What do you mean?' Toby asked.

'I mean she likes you, silly. Don't you go telling her I said so, will you?'

'I didn't really mean that,' he said. 'Why should I be cock-a-hoop? That's what I meant.'

'You haven't heard then, have you?'

'Heard what?'

' 'Bout that boy, that Hetherington. It was Mum that found him, at the bottom of the stairs. She don't like

51

him, I can tell you. He's rude, see. Treats her like a skivvy, and Mum don't like that.'

'Hetherington? What about him?'

'He fell down the stairs. Twisted his ankle, Mum said. That Mr Price was there, and then I seen him by the notice board with that Hunter and they were talking about you. Hunter said he thought you were about as good as Hetherington anyway and Mr Price wrote your name up on the team list. I seen it.' Before he could say anything he saw Hunter and Runcy coming towards him.

'Hetherington's twisted his ankle,' said Hunter. 'You're in the first team this afternoon. Well don't just stand there, you'd better go and clean your boots. And clean laces too. Pricey gets ugly if you've got dirty laces.' And then he spoke to Wanda. 'You coming to the match this afternoon?'

'I might,' said Wanda, shrugging her shoulders, 'if I've got nothing better to do.' And she walked away from them. Then she turned and walked backwards for a bit. 'If I do, will you win?'

'Course we will,' said Hunter, 'now that Jinks is in the team.' And Wanda turned and ran off up the steps towards the kitchen. Toby felt a pang of jealousy. 'Right Jinks?' Hunter was talking to him like a friend. The jealousy had evaporated instantly.

'How come,' said Runcy, 'how come you're always around her?'

'Ask a silly question,' said Hunter. 'It's 'cos she's pretty, isn't that right Jinks?' And he put an arm round Toby's shoulder as they walked off with Runcy, and Toby felt as if he'd just joined the Three Musketeers. 'Bit of a miracle, really,' Hunter went on. 'Couple of hours before the match and Hetherington goes and crocks himself, and there you are in the team. Still, that's how it goes. Keep the passes long and low remember, and in front of me. I don't like passes behind me.'

They left Toby standing in the quad and within seconds he was surrounded by hoards of small boys congratulating him. And then it came to him – Christopher's miracle!

This was the miracle he had been promised, and until Hunter had said the word and until the word had sunk in he hadn't even realised it. He saw Christopher coming through the throng of boys, hand outstretched and smiling. 'Well done, Toby,' he said, taking his hand and squeezing it. 'Good luck this afternoon.' Toby could not manage a single word in reply. He looked at him and saw that it was all true. Christopher *had* seen Jesus in the camp in the park. He was Jesus. He was the Son of God. He must be. He had worked a miracle. In that moment Toby's doubts vanished.

Toby played that afternoon like a terrier. He barked around the base of the scrum, pouncing on the ball. He tackled ferociously and threw out the long low passes

Hunter wanted. At half time, muddied from his boots to his hair, he sucked his slice of orange and felt like a warrior. He looked across the pitch and saw Wanda standing under the Tree of Heaven in her raincoat. He waved at her and saw her smile back at him. He couldn't see him, but Christopher would be somewhere there too in the line of spectators. He would play the second half for Wanda and for Christopher.

They won the match easily by two Hunter tries to none. Even Rudolph came up to Toby and shook his hand and Pricey was beside himself with joy. 'I can't believe it,' he said, clapping him on the back. 'First time we've beaten St Jude's since I've been here. Brilliant, you were boyo, brilliant.'

The long trek back to school from the playing-fields, through the gardens and across the drive was a triumphal march. Hunter's arm around his shoulder was enough of an accolade in itself. He loved all of it, every word of congratulation, every ruffle of his hair. He looked time and again for Wanda but he couldn't see her. At supper that evening he went into the kitchen, ostensibly to fetch the bread. Wanda was leaning against the sink smoking a cigarette. 'Proper little hero, aren't we?' she said, smiling at him. 'Here, you can have a puff. It's all right, no one around. Mum's gone home and left me to do the dishes.' Toby took one quick puff, not because he wanted to – he hated the smell of cigarettes –

but he did not want her thinking he had never done it before. There was lipstick on the cigarette, he could taste it. He handed back the cigarette and tried to suppress the cough rising in his throat. He could not. When Wanda laughed he could do nothing but laugh with her. Still laughing she filled up his bread-basket. He was about to leave when she caught him by the shoulder. 'Toby,' she looked down at the bread and arranged it neatly in the basket for him. 'Toby, have you ever had a girlfriend?'

'No,' he muttered.

'Well, you have now.' And she bent over and kissed him on the cheek.

Toby felt Wanda's kiss for the rest of the evening. Indeed as he lay there in the dark of The Pit he wondered which miracle Christopher had been responsible for, the twisting of Hetherington's ankle or Wanda's kiss in the kitchen. Maybe it was both. Christopher was tugging at his blankets. Toby looked across. 'Tomorrow,' whispered Christopher, 'in the camp after letter-writing.'

'All right,' Toby said. And he wondered then not what he would be writing in his letter home but what he would have to leave out. He never told them anything he knew they wouldn't want to hear about. He edited his letters home so that they would think he was happy and always doing well, all the triumphs, none of the disasters.

So his letter the next day never mentioned he was 'on report'. It was a ball by ball commentary on the rugby match against St Jude's. It covered four sides and was the longest letter he'd ever written home. When he'd finished, he read it through and tried to imagine the smiles around the kitchen table when they heard he'd played in the First Fifteen. Gran would smile and maybe cry – she always cried when she was happy. His father would say nothing because he never did but he would go off to the office proud, and his mother would tell Mrs Marshall next door because she wouldn't be able to stop herself. Of course he never mentioned anything about Hetherington's twisted ankle – there seemed no point. Mr Birley read it without speaking. Then he put it down and took off his glasses. 'Well, Jenkins, your handwriting may be all over the place, and your spelling doesn't know where it's going, but when you want to write you write well, Jenkins. Off you go.'

He was still buttoning up his boilersuit as he ran down through the spinney and into the park. By the time he reached the camp and crawled in, he still hadn't finished doing up his belt. Christopher was waiting for him. 'Now do you believe me?' said Christopher.

'Yes,' Toby replied, and he meant it.

'You believe I am the Son of God, the second Jesus?'

'Yes.'

Christopher went on: 'So you won't ever doubt me again, no matter what anyone says, no matter what happens?'

'No,' said Toby, 'not after yesterday I won't.'

Christopher held out his hand and placed it gently on Toby's head. 'You are my first friend and my first disciple. Welcome brother.' The warmth of his hand made Toby shiver. Christopher was looking up at the roof of the camp. 'And this will be our secret place of prayer, our chapel. We'll build an altar here, over there where Jesus appeared to me.' The tone of his voice hardened. 'But you must never tell anyone what happened here. You must never tell anyone who I am. No one must ever know, unless I tell them. Swear before God.'

'I swear,' said Toby. Suddenly Christopher was on his knees, his hands together in prayer. 'Dear God, dear Father, I see all around me injustice, hunger, disease. I see people fighting each other all over the earth. Misery multiplies as greed multiplies. We have forgotten you. The Gospel of the Son of God is the same as it always was, that we should love one another. Only then will there be peace and joy on this earth. You have sent me, Father, to bring once again the same message of hope; and I promise that from this church of leaves and branches your word will go out all over the world. Peace on earth, goodwill towards all people. Amen.'

There was such passion in his prayer, such commitment. Every word he uttered left Toby ever more convinced that Christopher must indeed be who he claimed he was. Toby knelt down and prayed beside him, not because he felt he had to but because he wanted to.

They spent the rest of that Sunday afternoon building an altar in the rhododendron chapel. It was a laborious process, carrying in the logs from the spinney. By the time the quad bell rang for supper they had found a couple of corn-sacks and laid them out over the pile of logs as an altar cloth, and Christopher had crafted with Toby's sheath-knife a crude wooden cross that he first kissed reverently and then placed on the altar. They stood back and admired it together. 'It's all we need,' said Christopher, and he went on: 'Father, bless this place and give faith to all of us who gather here to pray to you.'

Toby waited a while before he spoke. 'Will there be others then, I mean besides you and me?' He paused. 'If you tell anyone else, they won't believe you, I know they won't.'

'You didn't believe me, not at first did you?' Christopher said, 'and nor will they, but they will in time, just like you did. When the time is right I'll choose who to tell, but meanwhile you and I will bind ourselves together as blood brothers in Jesus. Let me have your knife again.' Toby unclipped his sheath-knife from his belt and handed it over, hilt first. He looked on as Christopher felt the blade with his thumb. 'Still sharp,' he said. 'It's better if it's sharp.' Then there was blood trickling down from his forefinger into the palm of his hand. 'Your turn,' Christopher said, and he took Toby's right hand in his, turned it palm uppermost and drew the blade slowly across his forefinger. Toby watched his own blood run out and wondered why it was not hurting. Before he knew it, Christopher was pressing their two fingers together. 'Blood brothers for ever,' he said. And when Toby looked up into his eyes he found he could not look away. 'You are in me,' said Christopher, 'and I am in you.' At that moment a browsing cow stuck her head in at the entrance to the camp and chewed her cud at them. The quad bell was still ringing, and Toby's finger was beginning to throb.

'We'd better be getting back,' said Toby, trying to put a brave face on it. 'They'll put us in detention else.' Suddenly he wanted to be gone, to be out of this place, to be free of Christopher, but he knew somehow he never could be.

Toby's finger would not heal. It was the index finger of his writing hand and for some days afterwards it opened and bled every time he had to write. If he got knocked in rugby it always seemed to be on that finger. In the end it began to turn puffy red, then yellow along the cut, and he went to Matron for a plaster.

'A sheath-knife I suppose,' she said, putting his finger under the hot tap and holding it there forcibly. Toby winced and bit his lip to stop himself from crying out. 'Why they let you young savages have knives I cannot imagine. I mean really, what did you think you were doing?'

'Just whittling, Matron,' said Toby.

'Making a spear, I suppose.' Toby nodded. 'See,' said Matron, smiling. 'Savages, savages, just like I told you.' She dipped some lint in iodine and laid it round his finger. It was cold and comforting. Matron, for all her brusque toughness, had a gentle touch.

The pink plaster reached half way down his finger which was now twice as big as before and Toby was able to flaunt it and use it. If he couldn't finish his prep – it was his finger. If he hadn't washed his hands before lunch – it was his finger. If he was late into class because he couldn't do up the buckle on his sandals – it was his finger. Like everyone else Wanda wanted to know all about it too. 'You should be more careful,' she said. 'Can spread, that can, all the way up your arm and into your blood. Blood poisoning. We've had a cow die of it on the farm. Honest.'

And she went on to tell him all about other diseases you can catch on the farm, and then about her father's ram that had jumped in with the ewes at the wrong time of the year and so they'd be having lambs before Christmas now, and how he was furious with her and said it was her fault because she left the gate open when she hadn't. It was a monologue that lasted until they reached the gate that led out of the playing-fields on to the village road. Toby opened the gate for her. 'Do you want to kiss me again,' she said, 'or do you want a cigarette?' Toby took the kiss and smelt the baked beans she had cooked for their supper in her hair. 'Hope your finger gets better,' she said, and went off into the dusk.

Christopher never said a word about the plaster on Toby's finger, not until that night when everyone else in The Pit had gone to sleep. 'Toby,' he whispered, 'you should have told me about your finger.'

'Went poisonous,' said Toby.

'I know. I could have healed it for you. Is it better?'

'No, worse if anything.' Toby could feel it throbbing.

'Then I shall heal it,' said Christopher.

'But how?'

'Hold your hand out towards me. Closer,' said Christopher. Toby felt his hand taken and held for a brief moment.

'You can heal?' Toby whispered.

'If you believe I can, then I can. Goodnight Toby.' And the hand was withdrawn. Toby tucked his arm back under the blankets and felt his finger. It was still throbbing – it always throbbed worse at nights.

He laid there in the dark and tried to believe in Christopher's healing powers. He kept saying to himself over and over again, 'I believe, I believe, I believe,' but he couldn't concentrate long enough or hard enough to be sure that he really believed he believed. So he tried to pray for more faith, but Wanda's smiling face kept breaking into his prayers interrupting them. Instead he tried to think deliberately for someone to pray for, someone whose face he could picture in his head. He prayed for Gran in her wheelchair. He prayed that her Parkinson's disease would go away for ever, that her shaking would stop, and that she could be smiling and happy again. He was wondering who Parkinson was when he fell asleep.

He was still half-asleep at breakfast when Matron tapped him on the shoulder. 'Come and see me after breakfast. I want to change that dressing of yours.' When, half an hour later, she pulled it off in the surgery, she frowned and bent to look at it more closely. 'I always knew I was a good nurse, but this, though I say it myself, this is unbelievable, unbelievable. Will you look at that!' Toby looked at his finger. There was scarcely a mark on it. All the swelling had gone, the yellow had gone and the cut had closed almost completely. 'Well, there's no need to waste any more time on you,' Matron said. 'Off you go, and don't go messing around with that knife of yours. Silly child.'

Toby was still examining his finger, marvelling at it as he went downstairs. Christopher passed him going the other way. 'Better is it?' he said, and he never even waited for an answer. He knew already. Toby was sure of him now, quite sure. There was nothing Christopher

62

couldn't do, nothing he didn't know.

Morning lessons passed without Toby even noticing, but he kept checking his finger to remind himself that what had happened had really happened. In geography, Pricey gave them a test on the tundra which was difficult for Toby because he couldn't even remember what the tundra was.

In Madame Lafayette's French lesson he couldn't concentrate enough to remember whether you put colour adjectives before or after the noun. All he could think of was his finger and Christopher, Christopher the second Jesus, the Son of God, Christopher the miracle worker, the healer. He found himself staring yet again at Christopher when the door of the classroom opened and Cruella came in. Everyone stood up and then sat down again as she waved them back into their seats. She bent over and whispered into Madame Lafayette's ear. Madame Lafayette nodded and then she was looking straight at him. 'Shenkins,' she said – she could never pronounce her J's properly. 'The 'eadmaster, 'e wishes to see you.' Toby stood up, a sickening weight of fear in the pit of his stomach. It would be his report card – that's all it could be. Someone had given him a black mark and he wondered which of the teachers it had been. He'd done nothing else wrong, or nothing anyone had found out about – so far as he knew. He felt Christopher looking up at him and took courage from the sympathy in his eyes. He felt his strength return and summoned up the presence of mind to look unconcerned as he followed Cruella out of the classroom.

'Come along into the drawing-room, dear,' she said quietly, an arm around his shoulder as they went up the Bloody Steps. Not the study, the drawing-room. No one goes into the drawing-room except for parents and staff. He'd never been in there in his life. Something was wrong, worse than wrong.

Rudolph sat in an armchair by the fire, a tea tray in front of him on a table. He motioned Toby to the sofa opposite and Cruella sat down beside him and took the tea-cosy off the pot. 'Tea?' she said, 'and how about a chocolate biscuit?' Rudolph said nothing as the tea was poured out through a silver strainer. He lit his pipe, brushed the tobacco off his tweed suit and sat back crossing his legs. Toby tried the tea but it was still too hot so he ate the biscuit instead. The silence was too long to be comfortable.

'Jenkins,' said Rudolph, getting to his feet and standing with his back to the fire. Toby felt Cruella take his hand. 'Your mother rang me this morning and she asked me to tell you . . . she wanted to say . . .' He cleared his throat, coughed and looked away.

'Jenkins,' said Cruella beside him, 'Jenkins, it's your grandmother dear, she died, last night. I'm very sorry, dear. So sorry.'

CHAPTER 4

THE RIVER RAN SOFTLY OVER THE STONES. A SHOAL of silver parr bunched, hesitated, and then vanished suddenly under tresses of shifting green weed. Toby waited for them to emerge the other side into the sunlight but they never did. He reached down into the water and was about to shake the weed but he decided against it. The fish were lying doggo somewhere and did not deserve to be disturbed. Besides, he had his big fish to catch. Upstream a heron croaked in alarm and lumbered into the air making for the high elms in Innocents' Copse. His big fish rose again and thrashed in the dark pool under the overhanging alders and left behind it ever-widening rings of ripples. Toby had tried for this fish half a dozen times at least – a large brown trout, he was sure of it, and a wily one at that. He would try one last time before he moved on. He checked his fly was secure, a 'march brown' Rudolph had called it. 'I never use anything else this time of the year,' he'd told him.

It had all been Cruella's idea, not Rudolph's. 'You'll need time on your own, dear,' she had said. 'Time to get over the shock. A long walk perhaps, or fishing maybe. Do you like fishing? Henry, he could have your rod for the day, couldn't he? And I'll get Mrs Woolland to make up a nice picnic for you, how would that be?' Toby liked the idea, he liked it a lot. He'd miss French and geography and Latin. Rudolph looked none too happy about lending his rod, but after a bit of a bluster about what a fine fishing rod it was – 'split cane, ten foot long, best rod on the river' – he agreed. He let Toby have a box of flies, a priest, a net, and his map of the fishing. He spread the map out on the table and stabbed it with his finger. 'I've got the fishing all along the bottom of the park, from the brook here to the old ash there, the one that blew up in the gale last year. And that's the best pool, under the alders. Difficult to fish this side, a lot of branches in the way. Take care you don't get caught up. And Jenkins, don't cross over. Village fishing on the other side. They stay their side, we stay ours – you know the rules. You can go in the river but you can't cross over.'

Toby knew that much already. Every boy in the school knew you never ever crossed the river. The first thing you did as a new boy was to walk the bounds with Rudolph – the road behind the sports field, the spinney beyond Madame Lafayette's cottage, the brook, the river and the iron fence up to the road again. You go out of bounds and it was the cane. Toby was thinking about the cane. He'd only been up the red carpeted steps into Rudolph's flat three times in his four years at the school. Twice was for the cane and once was this morning, to the drawing-room, to be told that his grandmother was dead. Given the choice, he decided on balance that he would prefer to have the cane. When you had the cane you had it with other people usually. You suffered together. You felt sick. It hurt and you cried. It was somehow simple and straightforward and something everyone had to go through. He had tried to cry about his grandmother, but he couldn't. He knew he ought to be more upset, but he wasn't. All he cared about at this moment if he was honest with himself was catching that brown trout. He tried to picture Gran dead in her chair and wondered if that was where she died, or had it been in her creaky bed down at the end of the passage beside the photograph of Grandfather that she kept on the bedside table? He wondered if that was the last thing she looked at and hoped it was. He'd never known Grand-father but he looked kind in the photograph. He tried to make himself cry, forcing the tears out of his eyes, but they refused to come.

He picked the weed out of the march brown fly and shook it off his fingers. At least, he thought, at least she won't be trembling any more. She won't cry any more because she drops tea cups or because she's too weak to push herself up out of her chair to go to the toilet. And then he remembered his prayer of the night before. Hadn't he asked for the shaking to stop? Hadn't he prayed again and again that she could be free of it and happy and smiling like she was before? And hadn't his prayers been answered?

Gran had gone to heaven and was happy. He wouldn't see her again, not for some time anyway, but she was happy and she wasn't shaking any more. There was no Parkinson's disease in heaven. It was then that he felt the tears filling his eyes at last. He welcomed them and sat down against the trunk of the old ash tree and cried out loud, the tears rolling into his mouth so that he could taste their saltiness.

He heard something moving behind him. He didn't bother even to look at first for he knew what it would be. There were cows browsing in the park. He turned now to be sure they weren't too close – he was always a bit wary of them. They had a wild and wicked look in their eyes. But it wasn't the cows. He was surprised to see Wanda coming down past the swimming-pool. He turned away at once, brushed the tears from his face and tried to compose himself. 'Hello,' she said cheerily and she tucked her skirt underneath her and sat down beside him. For several moments she said nothing more. She took out a cigarette and lit it. 'I got the day off school – helping Dad – supposed to be. Mum said you'd be down here,' she said. 'Want a puff?' Toby shook his head. 'My Nan died,' she went on, 'last Christmas. Christmas Day it was. I never liked her much and she didn't like me, but it don't matter do it? I still miss her. Cancer. She had cancer. I've got this ring.' She held out her hand to show Toby and waggled her fingers. 'It's gold. Honest. Left it to me she did. You like it?' Toby tried to smile but he wasn't very good at it. She put her hand on his arm. 'You want me to go away do you?' Toby shook his head. 'You caught anything yet?' she said, noticing the rod lying in the grass. And he told her then of his long duel with the big brown trout under the alder trees.

'I keep getting caught up in the branches,' he said. 'You know, when you cast.' And he demonstrated how it was done. Wanda smiled and got to her feet, brushing the grass off her skirt.

'If you want to catch anything in that pool you got to fish from the other side. Come on, I'll show you.' She held out her hand for him and hauled him to his feet. She kicked off her shoes and began to wade across the river. 'Don't forget the rod,' she said without looking back. 'It's cold, it's cold,' she squealed, and then she began to run.

Toby watched her skipping and splashing through the shallows. Just being with her had made him forget everything else. All thoughts of his grandmother had gone, all worries of breaking the out-of-bounds rule were of no consequence. He followed her across the river.

She used the rod so easily, like an extension of her arm, sending out the fly to land at the far end of the pool and allowing it to float back across. 'Benjie taught me,' she said reeling in slowly. 'That's my brother. Taught me to shoot and all. Can you shoot?'

'No,' said Toby.

'He snares rabbits, foxes. I don't like that. I told him, but he don't listen. Don't get me wrong, killing's all right, 's long as it's quick, long as you can eat it afterwards, that's what I say. Benjie, he kills anything that moves. Don't tell no one will you, but he does a bit of poaching on the side, you know a torch and a gaff, brings back whopping fish.' She looked at him and smiled. 'And he don't like you lot up at the school neither. "Toffs" he calls you, 's what we all call you. You call us "oiks" don't you?'

'Only sometimes,' Toby admitted it reluctantly.

'You think I'm an oik do you?' said Wanda, bunching the line in her left hand.

'Course not,' Toby insisted and when he ventured a look at her he found her still smiling at him.

'Yes you do,' she said, 'but it don't matter.' And she cast out again. 'You're all right, Toby,' she went on. 'Like I told Benjie, there's nice toffs and nasty toffs. You're a nice toff, and anyway, you're my toff aren't you? I'm your oik and you're my toff, and I've caught a fish! He's on, he's taken it! He's a big 'un Toby, a fighter!'

The line suddenly tightened, weed dangling and dripping all along its length. The reel rasped as the line ran out. Wanda reeled in gently and shouted for Toby to fetch the net. He'd left it on the opposite bank. He floundered across the river, found it and floundered back again. One slippery, shifting stone was enough to send him face down in the river. When he picked himself up he was soaked from head to foot and his wellingtons were full of water. Wanda pealed with laughter as he squelched up the bank towards her. The fish was only a few feet from the bank now its tail flailing in a last desperate effort to break free.

Wanda, still laughing, took the net from him, scooped the fish out of the water and emptied it on to the bank. She dispatched it quickly, one blow with a stone to the back of the neck. She took the hook from the mouth and sat back on her heels admiring the fish.

'That's not a brown trout,' she said. 'That's a sea trout.' She grinned at Toby. 'Fancy a bite to eat?' she said.

She made a small fire from the driftwood they found on the stony beach opposite the fishing-hut. She gutted the fish with Toby's sheath-knife, skewered it and turned it slowly over the fire. Toby sat watching in his shirt and shorts – everything else, his boilersuit, his socks, his tie and his belt were laid out in the sun to dry, his upturned wellingtons beside them. They ate the fish in silence, pulling the flesh from the bones with their fingers and then licking their fingers until there wasn't a taste of it left. Wanda opened up the sandwiches she had made for Toby that morning and shared out the lettuce and tomatoes between them. She chucked the bread into the river. 'For the fish,' she said.

Lying out in the sun afterwards Wanda lit a cigarette and blew smoke-rings up towards the sun. Toby looked across at her. He wanted to ask her but at the same time did not want her to think him ridiculous. He found the courage and asked her. 'Wanda? Do you believe in God, you know in Jesus, in heaven and all that?'

'Course,' said Wanda. 'Not just an accident are we? We've got to come from somewhere, and if we come from somewhere, like as not we go back there afterwards.'

Toby was encouraged and went on: 'So your nan and my gran, they're up in heaven.'

'Well, I don't know about my nan,' said Wanda, 'wicked old stick she was. Drunk a lot, swore a lot. She weren't no angel. If she got to heaven then it weren't by much.'

'And what about Jesus,' said Toby. 'Do you think he's real?'

'I suppose,' said Wanda.

'It says in the Bible,' said Toby, 'it says he'll come back one day.' Toby would probe as far as he could. 'Do you think he will?'

'Well I don't know, do I?' said Wanda, smacking a horsefly off her leg.

'I think he will,' said Toby.

Wanda raised herself on to her elbows and looked down at him. 'You don't half say some funny things,' she said, and then she leant over and kissed him on the cheek. 'My little toff,' she said, and brushed the hair out of his eyes. The school bell rang out from across the park. Wanda sighed. 'I'd better go. Mum'll be after me. You'll be all right now will you?' She was on her feet now and walking away, talking as she went. 'Your gran, did she play cards?'

'Yes,' said Toby.

'So did my nan. Poker, gin rummy and that. Loved her cards she did. Maybe it's like you say, maybe they're up there now, your gran and my nan, and playing pontoon or something. God help your gran if they are.'

'Why?'

'Cos my nan's an awful cheat, that's why.'

Toby needed to say what was in his heart. He wanted to say it and he would say it. Wanda was wading back across the river. 'Wanda,' he called out. He was going to say that he loved her, that's what he was going to say.

'Yes?' she said.

'Thanks,' said Toby, 'for the fish I mean.'

'Little toff,' she laughed, and she picked up her shoes and ran off across the park.

Toby watched her until he could see her no more, until he was quite sure she could not hear. 'I love you,' he shouted. 'I love you.' And the echo died along the valley and left him alone. He thought then of going back up to the school. Everyone would know about his grandmother by now. When Simpson's brother had been killed in the Korean War the year before Simpson had basked for weeks in everyone's sympathy – they had even prayed for him in chapel. Toby had never liked Simpson much, but after the news of his brother came through he had to force himself to pretend to like him for a while. Of course it didn't last for long, but for a few weeks no master ticked Simpson off, no prefect bullied him, he had no detentions and he had a lot of new friends.

Toby was in two minds. On the one hand he wanted to go back up to school now to feel that glow of sympathy, to revel in his sudden popularity even if it was to be temporary; but on the other hand if he stayed in the park he would miss double-Latin – and he'd only half done his prep and it was untidy and he'd get hell for it.

No, he would stay. After all he would still be able to reap the benefits of his grandmother dying whenever he appeared, now or later. This way he could have his cake and eat it. He would do some more fishing. He would catch a fish for Wanda. She would like that.

He tried to imitate Wanda's casting style, keeping his arm stiff and straight as he brought it past his ear, but either the fish were not there or he did not have her magic. He caught lots of weed but no fish. He would cast just once more and then move on further downstream and try another pool. 'Come on little fish,' he said out loud. 'Come and have your din-dins.'

'Your din-dins,' echoed a mocking voice behind him. Toby turned. There were a dozen of them, maybe more, village boys; and the way they were laughing at him was not at all funny. One of them – Toby presumed it was the one who had just spoken – was coming towards him. He had a red kerchief around his neck. There was a tattoo on his forearm, a red heart and intertwining snakes.

'Din-dins,' he said and he snatched the rod out of Toby's hand. 'Looks like the toff's after our fish for his din-dins. What do you think you're doing Toff, eh? You're on our side. This is our side.' And he pushed him backwards repeatedly. 'You lot, you think you own the whole bloody world don't you?'

'Here, look at this, Benjie,' said another of them crouching down by the fire. He held up the fish-bone by the tail. He came over and gave it to Benjie who dangled it in front of Toby's nose.

'Well, well, well, we've got ourselves a little toffee-nosed poacher.' So this was Wanda's brother. It was hard to believe, but it could be his only way out. Toby swallowed the fear in his throat and found his voice. It sounded shrill, but he could do nothing about that.

'Wanda, she said I could,' he began. 'She brought me across. She caught the fish, not me. Honest she did.'

Benjie's face darkened.

'You leave her out of this,' he snarled.

'She's my friend,' said Toby.

'Friend, what do you mean, friend? Just because she skivvies for you up at the big house, that don't make her your friend.' He pushed Toby in the chest again, but harder this time so that Toby sat down on the ground, the breath knocked out of him. He felt angry and silly and frightened all at the same time.

'She's your sister, isn't she?' Toby saw the others gathering around him. 'You're Benjie, aren't you? She told me all about you. She said you taught her how to fish.'

'She told you that?' said Benjie.

'Yes, and all about your nan, how she died on Christmas Day and she liked playing cards and that.'

'Let's do him,' said someone from behind him, and Toby found his elbow kicked away from under him so that he was flat on his back and helpless. He shielded his eyes. He looked up at them, the circle of their heads a dark halo around the sun. One of them was crouching down behind him and before Toby could pull his head away he was caught by his ear. Toby cried out as he felt the skin tear. Someone spat at him. 'Stinking little toff.' 'Poacher!' 'Thief!' 'Let's duff him up.' Toby gripped the hand that had hold of his ear and tore it away. They were all around him now, there was no way out. Instinctively, he curled himself into a ball, his knees drawn up, his hands over his ears – he'd done it often enough when he'd been caught in the middle of a rugby scrum. He closed his eyes and braced himself for the first kick. They were yelling now, egging each other on; and the kicking, when it began, struck his shin and then his back and then his arm.

Benjie was shouting. 'That's enough. That's enough. Leave him be.' And Toby felt himself dragged to his feet. Benjie towered over him, still holding him by the scruff of his neck. 'You Toby are you?' Toby nodded. Benjie seemed to be searching for the words. 'She said you were all right.' He turned to the others. 'Wanda, she says he's all right.' And then back to Toby again. 'But that don't give you no right to come fishing our side. Just 'cos she's a friend of yours don't mean you can take liberties, you understand me, Toff? We're letting him go.' There was some murmuring. 'I said we're letting him go.' He pulled

Toby closer to him so that Toby could smell his breath. 'But just so as you won't ever do it again Toff, watch this.' And he pushed Toby away from him. He picked up the fishing rod in both hands, held it up in front of Toby's eyes and then brought it down over his knees, snapping it in two. 'Don't you never come over this side, d'you hear? And you tell your toffy friends what happens if you do.' They laughed at that and Benjie threw the rod down at Toby's feet and laughed with them. Toby bent to pick it up. When he looked up again one of them was dancing around with his boilersuit held up in front of him, another was doing up his tie, another his belt and they were tiptoeing around each other, pushing their noses up in the air. 'Top hole!' they chorused. 'La-di-da!' and 'Anyone for tennis?' Others were hurling his wellingtons at each other. Only Benjie was not joining in. 'You'd best be on your way,' he said, his voice lower now, more confidential.

'What about my things?' said Toby.

Benjie took him roughly by the arm and frog-marched him to the river. 'What's the matter with you?' he said. 'You want them to get nasty again, eh? Do you? Well, do you? Now get out of here.' And he pushed him so that Toby staggered backwards into the water. Behind Benjie he could see one of them climbing into his boilersuit and trying to pull it up over his shoulders. He was too big for it and couldn't do it up. 'Who's for din-

dins?' they mimicked. 'Din-dins, din-dins.' A sudden rage overwhelmed him. He'd show them. He'd show them. But he had to get past Benjie first. He made a dash for it but Benjie caught him by the wrist and dragged him back down into the river. 'You silly little beggar,' he said. 'You got no brains, you got no sense.' They were half-way across, Toby trying all the time to wrench himself free, when he looked up and saw the cows stampeding across the park. Out of the trees behind them came dozens of boilersuited boys charging down Woody Hill towards the river and screaming like dervishes. Benjie stopped and Toby felt the grip on his wrist loosen. He pulled himself free and ran for it. He must have stumbled several times to his knees for he was wet through by the time he reached the bank. Helping hands grabbed him and then they were all around him, Hunter, Porter, Simpson, Runcy, and asking him if he was all right.

'His ear's bleeding,' said Runcy. 'The oiks. They did it, didn't they?'

Toby nodded. 'I was fishing,' he said. 'They broke Rudolph's rod. He'll kill me.'

'We'll kill them first,' said Porter, and he bent and picked up a stone. Benjie was still standing in the river looking at them and the other village boys were coming down to the river's edge behind him. For some moments the two sides said nothing. They glared sullenly and silently at each other across the river.

Benjie spoke first, 'He came across our side. He shouldn't have come across. He was poaching our side.'

'So?' said Hunter, stepping forward. 'So? What did you want to go and beat him up for?'

'Hardly touched him,' said Benjie. 'Just taught him a little lesson so's he wouldn't come across again, so's none of you would. What you want to come to our side for, haven't you got enough of your own? All them football pitches, tennis courts, swimming-pool. Ain't that enough for you? This side's ours, you understand? You keep your toffy-noses on your side and you won't come to no harm.'

The chant around Toby was a murmur at first, then it became rhythmic and swelled. 'Oik, oik, oik, oik. Oik, oik, oik, oik.' The crescendo built slowly, and from the other side came the reply: 'Toff, toff, toff, toff. Toff, toff, toff, toff.' Toby looked around him, at the faces of his friends. They were contorted with fury, their eyes blazing, their feet stamping, their fists punching the air and he noticed that many of the fists held stones. He was about to join in the chorus and would have done so when he noticed Benjie looking straight at him. He was the only one on the other side not chanting. Gradually the chanting lost its rhythm as it was interrupted by a barrage of insults, lavatorial to start with, then an exchange of filthy invective, each side trying to out-do the other.

When the supply of insults was exhausted both sides reverted to the rhythmic chorus of hate in an attempt to shout each other down. It would have gone on for ever had not Benjie waved his hand imperiously over his head to silence his army. Hunter did the same and the river fell quiet again.

'His boilersuit, his things,' said Hunter, 'we want them back.' Benjie nodded slowly and then turned away and began to wade back through the river to his bank.

Toby did not see who threw the stone. He saw it hit Benjie on the head and he saw him go down on his knees in the water. Benjie felt the back of his head and then he was up on his feet again, unsteady. He turned and raked them with his eyes. Then he looked down at the blood on his hand, and backed away, breathing hard. 'Bastards, you asked for it,' he said. 'You bloody asked for it.' He bent down and almost with one movement picked a stone out of the river and hurled it. Behind him the village boys ran down on to the pebble beach, grabbed handfuls of pebbles and threw them, peppering the Redlands bank with a broadside of stones, many of which found their mark. Toby ducked but was hit on his neck, and then he found himself throwing stones with everyone else. They threw anything that came to hand, flotsam from the river, tin cans, clods of earth, sand, anything. When one of the village boys went down screaming and clutching his face a whooping cheer went up from the Redlands bank and the barrage from both sides intensified until both sides were being hit so often that they were forced to back away out of range.

They would dash in now in groups, pick up their stones, throw them wildly and then run back before they could be hit. Toby had made several such sallies and was dodging and weaving his way back up the beach to safety when he saw Christopher striding down across the park towards them. He was shouting something, but he was too far away and Toby couldn't hear what he was saying, not until he was closer.

'What are you doing? What's going on?' And then when he came right up to him, 'Toby, your ear, what's happened to you?'

Simpson did all the explaining that had to be done. 'They beat him up,' he said. 'They beat him up and they smashed Rudolph's fishing rod.'

'And they took his clothes,' said Porter, tossing a stone up and down in his hand. He took a short run and hurled it across the river.

Christopher looked around him for a moment at the battle and Toby saw there were tears running down his face. He ran forward to the river's edge. 'Stop it, stop it!' he cried. He was wading out into the river, the stones falling all around him. 'Stop it, stop it everyone.' He appealed to both sides, facing first one then the other, holding his hands up above his head and waving them.

Gradually the barrage subsided until at last there was silence. Christopher still held his hands in the air. 'Drop your stones,' he said quietly. 'Drop them and there will be peace.' He turned to Hunter. 'Your side first.'

'Why us?' said Porter. 'They started it. They beat Toby up didn't they?'

'Do as he says,' Hunter said. 'Someone's going to get hurt.'

The Redlands boys dropped their stones, Porter hanging on to his until last before hurling it angrily into the sand at his feet. Christopher swung round and faced the village boys. 'Now you,' he said. 'It takes both sides to make a peace.' Benjie had a stone in his hand ready to throw. He looked at Christopher long and hard.

'All right,' he said at last. 'All right.' And he dropped the stone into the water and turned away.

'It's not all right!' Toby saw it was the one who had twisted his ear. 'It's not all right. No Toff tells me what to do. He wants them, he can have them.'

There was only one target now and he was very close to them. Toby watched as Benjie tried to stop them, but he couldn't. They ran past him throwing stones as they came and all of them were aimed at Christopher. The Redlands boys looked on for a few moments, stunned into immobility, and then they charged down the bank and into the water. Toby went with them and fell almost at once. On his hands and knees in the cold water he looked up. The village boys were running off, some of them already vaulting the fence into the field. They were carrying the broken fishing rod and one of them was waving his boilersuit in triumph. Benjie was clambering up the bank. He turned and looked, and then turned again and ran off after them.

Christopher was being carried out of the river and up the bank. By the time Toby reached him he was stretched out on the grass. There was a red weal on his forehead and his cheekbone was swollen and bruised. His nose was full of blood and his eyes were open, staring at the sky. Toby pushed Runcy aside and crouched over him. 'You all right Christopher? You all right?' Christopher nodded and propped himself up on his elbows.

'You're mad, Christopher,' said Hunter in genuine admiration. 'You're bloody mad.'

'Bloody stupid if you ask me,' Porter said, and he went on, 'that lot don't want peace, they want war, and they're going to get it.'

'They've got your boilersuit,' Simpson shouted from the river. 'And they've got Rudolph's fishing rod. What're you going to tell him, Jinks? Jesus, he'll kill you.'

'Jesus kills no one,' Christopher spoke so softly you could hardly hear him, 'but he dies a little every time you use his name like that. Jesus will protect you, he'll protect all of us if you'll only let him.' He turned to Toby as he sat up, wiping the blood from his nose. 'I'm sorry, Toby,' he said, 'about your grandmother I mean.'

'Me too,' said Hunter. And just for a brief moment Toby wondered what they were talking about, and even when he remembered he found he couldn't mourn any more.

As he walked back up to the school he was wondering only how he was going to explain to Rudolph about his precious fishing rod. 'What'll I tell him?' he asked Hunter.

'We'll come with you,' Hunter said. 'There's safety in numbers.' They would all go to see Rudolph together, and Hunter would do all the explaining. 'Best to come clean,' he went on. 'Well, almost clean. Better not mention anything about you crossing over. It'll be all right.'

Rudolph listened in silence, banging his pipe out on the palm of his hand. 'I see,' he said nodding, 'I see. That sounds to me very like Mrs Woolland's boy again. I'll go and see her. She'll sort him out. She'll put it right.' His brow furrowed. 'But you shouldn't have tangled with them, you shouldn't have got involved. That was stupid, stupid, you hear me?' The tirade that was building suddenly stopped. Rudolph sighed and shook his head. 'It makes me mad. This kind of thing, it makes me mad. It's not the rod. I don't mind so much about the rod, but I will not have my boys treated like this. I will not have it.' And he walked away still muttering under his breath.

Toby could see that he meant it. Rudolph really did like them and Toby had never understood that in him before. He had a strange way of showing it sometimes.

Later they all lined up to have their wounds dressed by Matron in the surgery. She was not at all pleased with them. 'You should grow up, the lot of you,' she said, and then to Toby, 'and you were the cause I hear, the *casus belli*, the Helen of Troy.'

'Matron?'

'Oh, never mind, Jenkins. You washed it properly did you, your ear, like I told you? I can't use plaster, awkward place, wouldn't stick.' She tipped up a brown glass bottle on to some cotton wool. 'Iodine,' she said. 'What would we do without iodine? You know what they're calling it in the staff room?'

'No, Matron.'

'The War of Jenkins' Ear.'

'1739 to 1741,' said Christopher from behind him.

'This'll hurt,' said Matron, and she was right.

CHAPTER 5

TOBY WASN'T THE ONLY ONE WHO HAD FORGOTTEN about his grandmother dying. No one ever mentioned it, neither did there seem to be any sign of that groundswell of sympathy that Toby had been expecting and was so looking forward to. The school was buzzing with other excitements. Toby found he had the most celebrated ear in the school and he was called upon repeatedly to give his account of the battle against the 'oiks' down by the river, blow by blow. Matron was right, they were calling it 'The War of Jenkins' Ear' and he liked that, but he soon discovered that he was not the real hero. Ever since Christopher had emerged from the surgery, a white bandage round his head like a Japanese kamikaze pilot, he had been mobbed by a flock of adoring small boys. Benedict Swann, seven years old and the smallest boy in the school, took to following him about the school quite uninhibited in his hero-worship. Toby saw him on several occasions tugging at his jumper just so that Christopher would look at him. Word had got about that it was Christopher who had saved the day, that it was the fury of the charge following his stoning that had driven the 'oiks' back to their side. But everyone did not tell quite the same story. Porter, Runcy and their friends proclaimed noisily that the 'oiks' had chickened out and been chased off, that they wouldn't dare show their faces again, 'not in a million years, not if they know what's good for them.' They said little or nothing of Christopher's part in it all.

By supper Toby was wearing his iodine yellow ear like a medal and relishing the acclaim. They were lining up in the corridor as usual outside the dining-hall, prefects pushing them into line, when Pricey came up to him, took him by his tie and pulled Toby towards him. Automatically Toby showed him his hands, front then back – everyone knew Pricey was a stickler for clean hands before meals. But he slapped away Toby's hands and ruffled his hair cheerfully.

'Listen Jenkins, you want to get yourself all busted up, then do it on the rugby field, there's a good boy, where it'll do us all some good, eh? Let's have a look then.' And he examined Toby's ear closely. 'Nasty,' he said. 'Still, you saw the blighters off, didn't you?'

'Yes, sir,' said Toby, and preened inside.

'Good for you, boyo,' Pricey said, moving away. 'We don't want their sort on our patch do we?'.

As they filed into the dining-hall teacher after teacher congratulated him on his war-wound, and even the few who did not entirely approve of what had happened could not hide a sneaky admiration. Madame Lafayette said that French children would not 'be'ave in such a way,' but as she said it she smiled in a way that told Toby he had risen considerably in her esteem all the same.

Only Matron remained unequivocally scathing about the whole incident, condemning it as 'childish' and 'silly'. 'I mean really, Jenkins, at your age, you should be ashamed of yourself.' She had a way of making him feel very insignificant.

At supper that evening the talk on Toby's table was all of 'The War of Jenkins' Ear'. Many of those who hadn't been there insisted that they had been, and those who had been there recounted their exploits in detail, capping each other's stories repeatedly, but much of it Toby knew to be imagined. Benjie – they'd dubbed him 'Biffo' – was talked of as a kind of oafish tattooed Goliath. In fact he was considerably shorter than Hunter. All the 'oiks' grew in stature and strength as the stories multiplied and the battle took on epic proportions. It soon became clear that Christopher's peacemaking attempts were not universally appreciated. 'If he hadn't stuck his oar in we'd have beaten them to pulp,' said Simpson, deliberately speaking loud enough so that Christopher might hear them at the far end of the table. Christopher, who had said nothing at all during the meal, did not react. He sipped his water and looked out of the window unconcerned, uninvolved. Toby longed for him to get up on the bench and tell them all who he was. If he hadn't been sworn to secrecy he'd have done it himself – or so he liked to believe. He yearned for someone else to believe in Christopher as he did, someone with whom to share the great secret. Jesus had come back. He was sitting at this table, in their school. If this was what God's Son looked like, Toby wondered, what would God himself look like? Older, that was obvious; so he tried to imagine Christopher old, very old, with a long white beard and skin like tissue paper; and then he found Christopher looking back at him, holding his eyes, drinking him in, reading his thoughts. Flustered for a moment Toby reached for his glass of water and knocked it over.

At the other end of the table Mr Birley seemed preoccupied. He hadn't yet noticed the spilt water, but Toby wanted him to notice. He needed an excuse, any excuse to see Wanda, he had to explain. He had to tell her how it had all happened.

'Please, sir,' he said, leaning forward. 'Please, sir, can I get a cloth, sir?' Mr Birley looked up vacantly and nodded.

As Toby walked down between the tables and out of the dining-hall he felt that everyone was looking at him and flushed to the roots of his hair. A brief glance towards the High Table confirmed it. Rudolph was looking him over, leaning his chin on clasped hands. He was suspicious – Toby could feel it, he was sure of it. Did Rudolph know he had crossed the river? How could he know? Who could have told him? Once outside the dining-hall door he ran for the kitchen. Inside he could hear Mrs Woolland, shrill with anger. Toby stood on tiptoe and looked through the glass pane in the door. Mrs Woolland was pouring the custard out of a huge saucepan into a line of waiting jugs and Wanda was following her along with a cloth wiping the spills from the sides of the jugs and from the worktop. The stewed rhubarb waited in glass bowls on the trolley. There was no one else in the kitchen. He pushed open the door. Mrs Woolland looked up, her brow furrowing as she saw who it was. She put the saucepan in the sink and ran the tap.

'Toby. Just the one I wanted to see.' She ran her hands under the tap and shook them on to the floor. 'Over here young man, I've a thing or two to say to you.' Toby caught Wanda's eye and tried to glean how much Wanda had told her. Wanda's eyes were red with tears, her cheeks stained. She turned away and wiped her face with the back of her hand. 'Now,' said Mrs Woolland, looking over her shoulder to make sure no one else was

91

about, 'what I got to say to you Toby goes no further than this kitchen, you understand? You was across our side of the river this afternoon, weren't you? And don't you bother to tell me otherwise neither. Wanda tried that, and I didn't believe her and I won't believe you neither. I know my Benjie, I know him inside out. There's a lot wrong with him – I know that – but one thing he ain't, he ain't no liar, never has been. He told me what happened, what went on down by that river this afternoon, and I believe him. Next thing I know, I've got His Majesty in there knocking on my front door. Village lads have been causing trouble, he says. They broke his fishing rod, he says, beat up his precious boys and what was I going to do about it, and if I couldn't put it right then he'd have to take it to the police. Well I told him straight. I said first I'd ask about a bit and then I'd put matters right. And that's just what I done. Seems His Majesty only knows half the story, the half that suits him, if you know what I mean.' Toby knew well enough. 'Wanda here, after a bit of encouragement, she tells me her tale and I listens, all about her taking you across the river where you ain't allowed, and catching the fish. "It were my fault," she says – and she's right. "Don't tell him, don't tell Mr Stagg," she says, "else Toby'll get beat." She's got a soft spot for you, young man, like I have; but I'm not letting my Benjie take all the stick, wouldn't be right, would it? No, I'll have to tell His Majesty the truth,

I says to myself, the whole truth and nothing but the truth; and then I remember about your gran. And I thinks to myself that you've got hurt enough for one day already. So I decided, I'm not telling him nothing about you going across the river, not this time. But I want no more of this fighting, you understand, no more of this name-calling, you hear me? Not good for any of us. I'll tell Benjie that he's got to pay for the rod – I'll dock it from his money – 'cos he shouldn't have done what he did. Two wrongs don't make a right, do they Toby? And I'll make sure you get your clothes back and that'll be an end of it, you hear me?'

'Yes, Mrs Woolland,' said Toby greatly relieved, but still trying to piece it all together.

'Well, don't just stand there, give us a hand with these custards.'

Together he and Wanda pushed the trolley back down the corridor towards the dining-hall. Wanda said nothing until they reached the door. 'You've got a yellow ear,' she said. 'Does it hurt?' Toby shook his head. She ran her finger up the side of a jug, wiping off a dribble of custard and then licked her finger. 'What you said, you know, when I went off this afternoon. What you said,' and she looked straight at him. 'I heard you.' And she pushed the door open with the trolley and wheeled it into the dining-hall.

Toby was sitting down again and staring at the puddle

of water on the table in front of him before he realised he did not have the cloth he was supposed to have fetched from the kitchen. Mr Birley hadn't noticed. He was gazing down into the bowl of rhubarb he had still to serve out. The boys were looking at him, waiting for him. Mr Birley was a world away. He seemed to be more and more vacant these days.

School assembly the next morning followed the usual pattern. They stood silent in the hall waiting for the staff to file on to the platform in their gowns. Major Bagley's gown was brown with age and tattered at the edges, an ancient wind-whipped battle standard. At the piano Miss Wicks, the assistant music teacher, waited and watched for the moment Rudolph reached his central throne on the platform and announced the hymn. Everyone looked forward to Miss Wicks' days at the piano. She didn't play very well, but she pumped the pedals with great verve and enthusiasm. Miss Wicks made assemblies bearable, even enjoyable for the boys and teachers alike, hitting discordant notes regularly and often launching into one more verse of a hymn than she needed to and then stopping in mid-verse, full of confusion. She did that this morning, and came to an embarrassingly abrupt halt, coughed and cleaned her glasses agitatedly.

During the prayers that followed it was difficult to suppress the sniggering and many failed, hiding their crime under their hands. Toby knew that the only way not to catch the giggles was to shut your eyes and pretend they weren't happening. He'd caught a glimpse of Simpson biting his knuckles. Another look and Toby knew he'd be giggling too. He tried to concentrate on the 'Our Father' and managed it. He would not open his eyes till all the prayers were over – it was the only way. And then he heard the words at the end of a prayer he'd been dreaming through: 'until His coming again. Amen.' He ventured a look at Christopher beside him, who was deep in prayer. He has come again! He has come again! The new Jesus is right here beside me and I am his disciple. I'm his St Peter! His thoughts ran on like this all through the prayers. Once they were over the boys sat up and waited for Rudolph to speak as he always did after prayers; and today everyone in the hall knew what it would be about.

'Yesterday,' he began, 'yesterday something very foolish happened. Some boys from this school became involved in a fight with local boys from the village. It is not the first time this has happened in my time here, but I wish it to be the last. Certainly there was provocation, but that is no excuse. Redlands boys do not and will not behave like a pack of roughs. I don't care who started it, you do not retaliate. They do not know any better; we do. In future I shall be forced to beat any boy who gets involved in this kind of thing. There will be no excuses, no extenuating circumstances.' He leant over the lectern, rocking it forward. 'Do I make myself perfectly plain?' He stood back and took a deep breath. 'Very well, very well. Jenkins, I shall want to see you in my study after this.'

Every head in the hall swivelled and Toby looked down at his feet, longing for the moment to pass. So, Rudolph did know he had crossed over. Mrs Woolland had told him. She'd said she wouldn't. She'd said. But then maybe, he thought, maybe it wasn't her after all; maybe someone else had sneaked on him. It didn't make much difference; the consequences would be the same.

Toby hoped it would be just two strokes, but he knew if you were caught breaking bounds that four was more likely. Perhaps Rudolph would take pity, on account of Gran. It wasn't likely. The waiting would be the worst part, the sweating behind the knees, the dry tongue, the nausea; then the lecture as he reached for the cane behind the roll-top desk in the corner of the study, and the stag's head would be gazing down at you from the wall. You had to kneel on the severed elephant's foot that served as a stool. There was the smell of the leather armchair you had to bend over, and then the burning pain. Toby stood in the hubbub of the milling boys and wished he was dead like Gran. Christopher was suddenly beside him, an arm around his shoulders, walking him across the emptying hall towards the Bloody Steps. 'It'll be all right,' he said. 'Have faith.' Then he was gone and Toby was alone.

Toby climbed the steps trying to have faith, but it was not easy. He sat down on the settle outside the study to wait. The grandfather clock with the sailing ship on the face read ten past nine. He read the face as he'd done before – anything to keep his mind off Rudolph's study. 'J. Edgecombe Fecit 1802 Bristol'.

'That was my great, great, great grandfather,' said Cruella coming out of the drawing-room and looking rather proudly up at the clock. 'John Edgecombe, the clockmaker. He made all sorts of furniture.' She closed the door of the drawing-room and came towards him. 'Well, Jenkins,' she said, 'I've had your mother on the phone this morning. She wants to have you home for the funeral, and Mr Stagg says it's all right. It'll be the day after tomorrow. I'll take you to East Grinstead station and your mother will meet you at Victoria.'

Toby went down the steps, his heart singing with relief and joy. Home, he was going home. Here was proof positive, if any more were needed, that Christopher was everything he said he was. Hadn't he said it would be all right? Hadn't he said?

Toby didn't even mind the Tuesday run that afternoon. It was driving rain as they all gathered in the drive, shoulders hunched against the cold. The wind tore at the trees and sent the leaves swirling down the drive. Benedict Swann was standing under the trees and crying, his hair flattened on his head, his ears and chin dripping.

Toby watched as Christopher walked over to him and crouched down so that he could talk to him face to face. Toby followed him. Swann was nodding, sniffling and trying to smile. 'He all right?' Toby said.

'He's fine,' said Christopher. 'I told him he can run with us. We'll look after him.'

The whistle went and the boys stampeded up the drive, pushing and shoving to get ahead of each other. Pricey always ran at the front. No one had ever yet beaten him home, not even Hunter – Pricey liked to brag about that. Behind them came Mr Birley on his bicycle, to 'mop-up' the stragglers. They were glad it was Mr Birley. Unlike the other masters, he didn't mind if you walked a bit, just so long as you kept ahead of him. Toby got into his stride beside Christopher. There was no hurry. All you had to do was finish, and there was always the chance he'd see Wanda, and that was worth a lot.

Toby found it didn't hurt nearly so much when you had someone else to encourage. Little Benedict Swann pattered along the wet road glancing up every now and again to see if Christopher was looking at him, and this Christopher did often enough to keep him going. They came into the village, passing the churchyard on the left, and took the short-cut across the village green – it saved you going round by the telephone box and any saving was better than none. Much to everyone's relief there were no village boys there today – there rarely

98

were when it was raining. Toby couldn't feel his feet below the ankles now and his fingers were curling up with the cold. They swung up the lane towards the village school.

From there on it was mostly downhill and easy. Toby had a map of it in his head, every telegraph pole, every postbox, every road sign, anything that marked off the distance, that sliced it up to make it more bearable, that brought you nearer to the end of it all. Toby was passing the school sign when he heard the shouting up ahead. He knew then what he would have to face and took precautions. He ran across to the other side of the road to get as far away as possible from the playground fence and it was just as well he did. As he came round the corner he saw the chain-link fence was crowded with village children, some laughing, some putting out their tongues, all of them shouting and jeering and whistling. Toby quickened his pace leaving Christopher and Swann some distance behind him. When he turned he saw that Swann was walking now and crying again. Christopher was beckoning him back to help and Toby ran over to him, put an arm round Swann and began to lead him away.

'Look after him,' said Christopher, and he walked over to the school fence and began to talk to the village children. Within moments the barracking had quietened and some were even smiling and laughing. A teacher came running out of the school across the playground. She was waving Christopher away as if he was a dangerous dog.

'Go away,' she shouted at him. 'Go on, go away. You don't belong here. You only cause trouble.' And then to her own children. 'Inside, inside. Wet playtime, wet playtime.' And she hustled them all away, looking over her shoulder and grumbling at Christopher as she went.

Mr Birley cycled up and stopped, glad of the rest. 'Christopher,' he said, trying to catch his breath, 'I saw that. What did you say to them?'

'Nothing much,' said Christopher, 'I was just friendly. I asked them if they wanted to come on the run and they laughed. I don't think they liked the idea very much.'

Mr Birley nodded and sniffed. 'No more do I,' he said. 'Trying to talk Mr Price out of his Tuesday run is not easy, not easy at all. Still, at least the rain's easing off a bit. That's something. You all right, Swann?'

'He's fine,' said Christopher, 'aren't you Swann?' And Swann smiled through the last of his tears and nodded. Toby looked out for Wanda as they trotted past the farm gate, but there was no one about. It was a hard run to finish.

The hot bath brought some feeling back to Toby's feet and hands, but even after that his thumbs wouldn't work properly when he tried to do up the buckles on his sandals. Matron had sent for him to fetch a spare boilersuit and some boots. He found her in the surgery and she was fuming.

Swann was shivering and whimpering in the corner of the surgery, he was sitting on Miss Whitland's lap, a thermometer in his mouth.

'Madness,' said Matron. 'Sheer madness. I've three in bed already. I shouldn't be surprised if they end up with double-pneumonia. If Mr Price wants to kill himself that's his business, but if he does this again I'll do the job myself. What is it about these overgrown schoolboys?' She looked at him. 'What do you want, Jenkins? Oh yes, you've come for your boilersuit, haven't you? His Majesty says you'll be getting your own one back in the next day or so. I'll believe it when I see it. Over there, over there.' And she waved him towards a neat pile of clothes and a pair of wellingtons beside it. 'And Jenkins, those are mine. Don't you go losing them this time or I'll get ugly, and you don't want me ugly, do you?'

'No, Matron.'

She went across to Swann, took out the thermometer and read it. 'Sick room for you,' and Swann sniffed back his tears. 'Believe me, I know how you feel,' said Matron, shaking the thermometer. 'Go on, Jenkins, don't just stand there. Off you go.'

Toby found Christopher where he hoped he'd find him. He was sitting in the rhododendron chapel reading his Bible. 'Swann's in the sick room,' said Toby.

'Then we'll pray for him,' said Christopher. Toby had never seen him so sad. 'We'll pray for all of us, for an end to this hate. Did you feel it this afternoon in the village? Did you see it in their eyes? How is it that people can hate each other like that? Why? What for? It's like a sickness, like a plague. Somehow I've got to cure it Toby, I've got to.'

They prayed together silently, kneeling in front of the altar. As usual, Toby found he had finished long before Christopher. He could never make his prayers last for long, no matter how hard he tried. He was just thinking that the boots he had borrowed from Matron were pinching him when a great shout went up outside in the park.

He left Christopher praying and went out. They were coming from all directions, running down towards the river where there was already a gathering of boys looking across at something on the other side. It was a Redlands boy. He was being held on both sides by two village boys who seemed to be hanging something around his neck. One of them looked like Benjie but Toby was too far away to be sure. He called Christopher.

'Looks like they've taken a prisoner,' said Toby, and together they ran down towards the river.

As they came closer they could see Benjie standing with his legs apart, hands on his hips. It was then that they saw that the boy in the boilersuit they were holding was not a boy at all but a scarecrow dressed up in a boilersuit, Toby's boilersuit, and it was wearing his tie and belt and boots. There was a notice written in red chalk on brown corrugated cardboard around the neck. It read TOFF. Benjie was shouting something at them but Toby couldn't hear what it was. Hunter waved everyone to silence. They could hear him now.

'Why don't you come and get it? I brought his things back just like I was told, but that's all I'm doing. I'm not getting my feet wet, not for a load of toffs.' Everyone was looking at everyone else.

'See.' said the other village boy, his thumb in his belt. 'Chicken, like I told you, they're chicken.'

'We're not chicken,' Hunter called back. 'We're not allowed to cross, that's all. I'll meet you in the middle.'

'Don't do it,' Porter whispered. 'It's a trap. You can't trust them.'

'I told you,' said Benjie. 'I'm not getting my feet wet. You want it, you're going to have to come and get it.'

'I'm coming.' It was Christopher. He was walking down into the river. In stunned silence they watched him wade across and climb the bank on the far side. As he reached the top the undergrowth shivered and suddenly came alive. A dozen, twenty, twenty-five village boys emerged and moved towards him. In an instant Toby found himself leaping down the bank with everyone else and charging through the river yelling his fury.

'No!' cried Christopher turning on them and holding up his hands. 'No!' And they stopped where they were, the river tugging at their legs.

He ignored the village boys and walked straight up to Benjie. 'Thank you,' he said, and then he reached out, took the label off the neck and gave it back to him. 'I think you'd better keep this,' he said. He picked the scarecrow up, tucked it under his arm and walked back through the river. Someone started cheering and then they were all cheering. They surrounded him and carried him out of the river and across the field. Toby could see he was begging to be put down, but no one would listen. Simpson and Runcy pulled the straw out of the dummy, and Toby found himself loaded with all of his missing clothes and his boots as he followed along behind the triumphant cavalcade. He looked round just once and saw Benjie and the village boys still standing, unmoving, on the far bank. And he knew then from their faces that this was not the end of it.

Cruella drove Toby to the station the next morning. She asked after his ear and said that the best thing was to avoid the local boys if they were going to be like that. 'It's like Mr Stagg said,' she went on, 'they just don't know any better. Mr Stagg was very upset, Toby. That rod was his pride and joy. Still, Mrs Woolland is as good as her word, isn't she? You got your clothes back like she said you would and Mr Stagg will be paid for his fishing rod,

I'm sure of it. She's a brick, our Mrs Woolland. They don't make them like her any more.' She didn't wait to put him on the train. She bought his ticket, handed him his brown leather case and took him to the platform. 'I have to dash back,' she said. 'Mr Birley's away today and I have to take his lessons. Poor Mr Birley, it's his little girl again, little Jenny. She's been in and out of hospital ever since she was born. Don't you worry, I'll be here tomorrow to collect you off the half-past-two train. You'll be all right now, will you?' And she was gone, hurrying away over the footbridge. Toby thought then that Cruella was not at all the right name for her. She was tall and she was thin, her legs like bean poles, more like Olive Oyl in *Popeye* than Cruella.

Toby loved to lean out of the carriage window and smell the smoke and feel the speed, but just outside East Croydon he got a smut in his eye and spent the rest of the journey trying to get it out. When his mother met him at Victoria she thought he had been crying. She comforted him on the platform, wiping his face with a handkerchief and telling him that he wasn't to be upset, that Gran hadn't suffered. She'd died in her chair listening to the radio, *Desert Island Discs*, her favourite. And we've all got to die sometime. She had a good long life. And then she cried herself and hugged Toby close. Toby breathed in the smell of her and closed his eyes. He was home. He didn't care about the funeral or about Gran. He was home for only a short time, but even a few hours away from school was better than nothing at all. Tonight he'd be in his own bed. For one day at least there'd be no bells, no lining-up, no detentions, no tests. He would make the best of it.

Gran was buried that afternoon in the graveyard of St Thomas' Church, just down the end of the road. It was raining hard and the noise of the rain on the umbrellas made it difficult to hear what the vicar was saying at the graveside. Toby couldn't help thinking of Gran inside the coffin. He didn't want to, but he couldn't help himself. 'Dust to dust,' the vicar raised his voice as the rain drummed on the coffin. Toby thought of Christopher. He'd ask him when he got back. He'd know the answer, he knew the answer to everything. If, like the vicar had said, we are dust to start with and we are dust afterwards, then where's the point in living? If Gran had come from heaven and now she's gone back there, then why does God bother to make us live on the earth at all? There was no sense in it, no sense at all.

Toby sat back in the sleek black limousine afterwards and stretched his legs. His father sat beside him in his heavy black rain-spattered coat, his shoes muddy and wet from the graveside. He kept blowing his nose and looking out of the window. No one spoke. You could hardly hear the engine. The chauffeur sat bolt upright behind the glass partition, so erect that Toby wondered if he had a stiff neck.

The family gathered back at the house for tea and sandwiches and Toby found himself playing waiter to all his uncles and aunts and cousins. Charley was about the only one not dressed in black. She scooted around the floor on her bottom, screeching until she found someone to play with her and then she quietened for a bit. If it hadn't been for her it would have been a grim affair. It was Charley who got everyone laughing, Charley who took everyone's mind off the empty chair in the corner. But it was Toby's ear that provided the main talking-point. His father proudly broadcast the story that Toby had told him – it was a rugby injury. Toby was in the First Fifteen now, scrum-half.

'Playing for England next I suppose,' said his Uncle Bob, picking through the sardine sandwiches till he found one that didn't have a crust on it.

'Shouldn't be surprised,' said Toby's father, his hand on Toby's shoulder. Charley screeched too loudly and had to be taken out, and the talk turned to Gran and it all went quiet again. Toby looked across to Gran's empty chair by the window and wondered if her ghost was sitting there watching him. He smiled at her in case she was. Already it was getting dark outside. At school, prep would be over and they'd all be out in the park. Christopher would be praying in the rhododendron chapel. For a moment Toby was tempted. He felt like telling everyone, shouting it out loud, that Jesus *was* true, that Heaven *was* true, so Gran would be there. She really would be. He wanted to tell them that Jesus had come back again, like he said he would, to save the world. 'And me, Toby Jenkins, I'm his first disciple!' He looked again at the empty chair. You know already, Gran, don't you? In heaven everyone would know by now, that Jesus was back on earth again, and that Toby was his Peter. They'd be talking about it. They'd be watching.

Toby's father came to see him in bed that night and asked him how his work was going, what books he had been reading, how high up he was in class order. Toby lied on all counts, because he had to, and when his father had gone out he thought again of the watching dead in heaven and maybe on earth, and hoped they had not been listening in.

No night had ever passed so quickly. No breakfast was over so fast, and Toby found himself back once again at Victoria Station, leaning out of the train window and waving goodbye to his mother, who turned and walked away down the platform, her fox-furs looking back at him over her shoulder. Toby hated the eyes on her fox-furs – they were mean little eyes, accusing eyes. Toby didn't understand why, but his stomach was not heaving with homesickness as it should have been. He pulled up the leather strap to close the window and sat down alone in his carriage. He had to admit it to himself, he was actually looking forward to going back. He longed to see Wanda, and Christopher too. He couldn't work out which of them was more important to him; and he felt bad about that because he knew it should be Christopher, and he wasn't sure it was.

Cruella was there to meet him on the platform in the same camel coat and green beret. Mr Birley was still off school she said, his daughter no better; and one of the chimneys was blocked with jackdaw nests. 'Mr Stagg says we'll have to send one of you boys up to clean it out, like they did in the old days.' Toby looked at her to be sure she was joking. He wasn't sure until she smiled at him. 'Not you, Jenkins,' she said. 'You're too big. We'll send little Swann up, shall we?'

'The boys will all be out in the park,' she said when they got back. So Toby donned his boilersuit and went looking for Christopher. He wasn't in the rhododendron chapel so he wandered on down towards the river. The park seemed strangely deserted. The cows grazed under the horse-chestnut trees at the far end by the brook and one of them looked up and lowed at him. And then he saw it. Standing near the fishing-hut was a scarecrow dressed in dungarees with a check shirt and a red kerchief around its neck. He recognised them at once – Benjie's clothes. There was a notice hanging round his neck. Toby didn't need to look for he knew what it would say. Something moved in the undergrowth behind the alder trees. It was Porter waving him over and then waving him down. There were others, Runcy, Simpson, dozens of them lying in ambush, some behind the fishing-hut and some in the long grass by the fallen ash tree. 'For Christ's sake,' Porter hissed at him. 'Over here, over here. They'll see you.' And then Toby noticed he had a long stick in his right hand. They all had them, and every one of them had been sharpened to a point.

CHAPTER 6

THE COWS WATERING IN THE DEW POND WERE
suddenly spooked and came galloping out from under
the trees, their tails high with alarm. At first Toby could
not see why they should be behaving like this. He put it
down to biting flies or a swarm of bees perhaps. He soon
saw that it was neither. Custer came bounding up out of
the pond and shook himself till he staggered; and behind
him, coming across the ramshackle bridge over the ditch
beyond was Matron. The cows had stopped by now. They
turned and faced the dog, their heads lowered. One or
two of them began to trot purposefully towards him,
skipping and tossing their heads. Matron waved her stick
and shouted at them, and they kept their distance. Custer
came gambolling on towards Toby, his tail circling in
welcome. He jumped up at once and slobbered on Toby's

arm, his pink tongue dripping. He had been rolling in something that smelt like a farmyard so Toby backed away at once and pushed him down. Rejection was not new to Custer, and he was not hurt by it. He simply looked around for other amusements and then ran off towards the fishing-hut where he pounced on a stick and carried it off proudly to Matron who ignored him. She had seen the scarecrow.

'Jenkins,' she said, pointing her stick. 'What on earth is that?' She had only to turn round and look and she must see them. Porter was cowering behind her in the undergrowth and Toby could make out at least five others lying face down in the grass by the fallen ash tree. Sooner or later Toby knew that Matron must see them. 'Cat got your tongue, Jenkins?' she said. Custer was whining and snuffling at the door of the fishing-hut. Matron called him, but he was too intent on the door to pay her any attention. She was standing right in front of the scarecrow now and reading the notice around its neck. 'Oik,' she said. 'It says "oik". Did you write this, Jenkins?'

'No, Matron.'

Custer was up on his back legs and scratching frantically at the door. 'What is he after?' She was frowning. There was a muffled cry from inside. 'Jenkins,' she went on, her voice calm and measured. 'I think there may be someone in His Majesty's fishing-hut, don't you?'

'Yes, Matron.'

'Then I suggest, Jenkins, that you go and open the door and let him out. I think that might be a good idea, don't you?' Suddenly she wheeled round. 'And I suggest Porter – yes, I can see you Porter, and you Runcy – I suggest that you and your silly friends stand up and show yourselves. You're like a bunch of ostriches. Do you hear me, Porter?'

Porter stood up sheepishly, his spear in his hand. 'All of you,' she said.

They stepped out from behind every bush, it seemed, and every one of them was clutching a spear. 'Jenkins, get that door open.' There was an edge to her voice now, an edge she used only rarely, but when she did you knew that her patience was wearing thin. Matron angry was a volcano and Toby felt an eruption was close. He was trying his best to pull back the bolt but Custer was scrabbling beside him, jolting the door and making it impossible for him to shift the rusty bolt. He pushed the dog down and kicked him away with his boot. 'Jenkins, the door!' Toby bent down, picked up a stone, and hammered furiously at the bolt until at last it flew back. He opened the door. Benjie was lying on the floor in his underclothes, a gag in his mouth, his wrists and ankles tied with binder cord. Toby tried to ignore the fury in his eyes as he knelt down beside him. He shouted at Custer to keep away and fought with the knots, cursing his bitten fingernails. In the end he had to use his teeth, but still he could not loosen the knots. It was only then that he remembered his sheath-knife. As he took it out Benjie shrunk back against the wall. Toby shook his head to reassure him, bent forward and cut the string. Benjie was on his feet in a flash, rubbing his wrists, pulling at his gag. He glared down at Toby and then ran barefoot out into the field. Toby followed him.

Several of the boys were kneeling down beside the scarecrow and undressing it, Porter amongst them. Matron was standing over them. She turned to Benjie, who was hugging himself. 'These your clothes, are they?' Benjie nodded. He looked much less formidable, Toby thought, in his vest and pants. 'Then you'd best put them on, hadn't you, else you'll catch your death.' Benjie snatched at his shirt and buttoned it with venom. He pulled his dungarees on and was sitting down tying up his boots before Matron spoke again. 'One guess,' she said, and she pointed her stick at Porter. 'You. You're behind all this aren't you, Porter? It's your speciality, this kind of nonsense.'

'But Matron . . .' Porter protested.

'And don't bother to deny it, Porter, it won't wash. Lying is so boring.'

'But Matron, we were just doing back to him what he did to us, what he did to Jinks.'

'Porter,' said Matron firmly, 'you will apologise to this

114

young man. At once, Porter, or I will take you to Mr Stagg and see what he has to say about all this.' Porter did not think for long.

'Sorry,' he mumbled, looking down at his boots.

'Louder,' said Matron, and prodded him in the stomach with her stick. 'So he can hear it.'

'I'm sorry,' Porter repeated grudgingly, louder this time.

'That's better,' said Matron, and then she turned to Benjie. 'I've seen you before haven't I? You're Mrs Woolland's boy, aren't you?'

'What if I am?' said Benjie.

'You came over into school grounds, didn't you? Is that what started all this?'

Benjie was fiercely indignant. 'I did not,' he said. 'I was fishing over on our side, that's all. They were waiting for me. They ambushed me, busted my rod. They dragged me over.' Matron was nodding.

'Did they now? Did they indeed?' And she reached out and took Runcy's spear. 'And what were these for? Playing Indians, were we? A little bit old for that, don't you think?' Porter looked away. 'Or were we planning a little ambush with the scarecrow as bait? Well, speak up, speak up.'

'Only for a joke,' someone mumbled.

'A joke? You sharpened these spears for a joke?' Benjie was on his feet and going. 'Before you go, young man.' Benjie stopped and turned around. 'Before you go I should like you to watch these boys throw their spears away into the river. You first Porter.' Porter hesitated, looking at the others for support. 'Do it, Porter, or it'll be the Bloody Steps and His Majesty's study for the lot of you.'

Porter walked to the river bank, threw his spear way down river and watched it float away. The rest followed suit, the spears chasing each other over the rapids beyond the fishing-hut and then out of sight.

'There we are,' said Matron. 'That's that then, that's an end of it. Do you understand? We want no more of this childish nonsense, do you hear me? I shan't say anything about it this time, but I tell you this much, if I ever hear of such goings on again His Majesty will hear all about it, and I think you know what that will mean, don't you?' And they watched her striding away through the thistles after Custer, who was trotting on ahead of her, an unwieldy stick in his mouth. 'And I want to see that ear of yours in surgery, Jenkins,' she called out, waving her stick in the air. Benjie barged through them and ran for the river. He hopscotched across from boulder to boulder and grabbed an over-hanging branch to haul himself up on to the bank. He faced them now, breathing heavily.

'We'll be back,' he shouted. 'Don't you worry, we'll be back. You asked for it now. You asked for it.' And

Benjie's last words still hung over them later that afternoon when the quad bell went and they tramped up through the park back to school. Hardly anyone spoke.

It was as if Toby had never been home, that the last twenty-four hours had been a twenty-second dream before waking up to the real world again. A pang of familiar homesickness tugged at Toby's stomach as he took off his boilersuit in the boot room. It was still with him as he climbed the stairs to the surgery. He tried to console himself with the thought that at least he could cross two days at once off his calendar that evening, two days closer to half term, two days nearer home. He wondered why he hadn't yet seen Christopher. He'd find him after he'd been to surgery. Just being with him would make him feel better – it always did.

Matron painted his ear yellow again. Her hands were cold as she tipped his face to one side to look more closely. 'I hope you weren't part of that silliness down in the park, Jenkins,' she said.

'No, Matron,' said Toby, thankful that he hadn't been. She was not easy to lie to.

'No, I didn't think so,' she said, but she said nothing more until she had finished. Toby was sitting on the stool facing the open sick-room door. 'Your friend's in there,' said Matron, washing her hands at the sink. 'Christopher,' she went on. 'I had to have the doctor in for him yesterday. Concussion, delayed concussion the doctor said it was, after that knock on his head. He keeled over out in the park somewhere, fainted clean away. Hunter brought him in, carried him all the way up. Strong as an ox, that boy.'

'Is he all right?'

'He will be, but the doctor said he'll be in bed for a few days, a week maybe. He's a strange one – the doctor said so too, not like a normal boy at all. Too good to be true almost. Still, makes a change from all you savages. You want to see him do you? Hunter's in there with him – he's always in there – and there's three of Mr Price's victims from the Tuesday run, so no noise, I don't want them disturbed.' Toby got down from the stool. He thought she'd finished. 'How was the funeral?' she said. Toby did not know quite what to answer. He didn't have to. 'If you ask me,' she went on, 'a funeral should be a party, something to remember. The Irish know how to do it. Over there you have a wake – you know, music, laughter, drinking, everyone's happy. How it should be. I'm Irish, you didn't know that, did you? Well, I am, and when I go I'll see they do the job properly. If they don't then I'll come back and haunt them.' She smiled at him. 'When you die, Jenkins, it's not the end of something, you know, it's the beginning, and that's something to celebrate, don't you think? So keep smiling, you hear me?' It was an order. Toby returned her smile and went into the sick room.

In the first bed he passed Benedict Swann was fast asleep, his cheeks flushed, his thumb deep in his mouth, his finger alongside his nose. Toby could not see who the lumps in the beds opposite were but whoever they were, they too were not moving. Christopher was beckoning to him from the bed by the window. He was propped up on a bank of pillows, the bandage still around his head; and beside him was Hunter who had a book open on the bed. Christopher put a finger to his lips and waved him into the chair opposite Hunter. Toby saw that the open book was a Bible – it was open at St Matthew. His eyes met Hunter's and he found a fellowship there that had not been there before. He turned to Christopher for confirmation of what he now suspected. 'Yes,' said Christopher, 'he's one of us now. I had another vision. Jesus told me, my voices told me that I should choose whoever was there beside me when I woke up – it was just the same with you.'

'He knows?' said Toby. 'He knows about you?'

Christopher smiled. 'Yes,' he went on, 'he knows. We are all brothers in the Lord. Blood brothers.' He took Hunter's hand from the Bible and laid it on the bed. There was a cut across his finger. Toby was torn inside. Hunter was one of them, he was with them, he was his brother now and, except for Christopher, there was no boy in the school he admired more; yet he felt suddenly envious that his place alongside Christopher was no longer unique, that he had been somehow usurped. He tried to banish such thoughts before Christopher sensed them. Christopher took his hand and laid it on Hunter's and then covered their hands with his. 'Between us,' he said. 'Between the three of us let there always be absolute trust. Bind us by faith, Father, and by love, and let nothing ever divide us. My voices have told me and I know now this is a prelude to the work I must do when I am older. This hate must be exorcised. I must do it before it is too late. Last time it was stones. Next time it will be spears. I know it. I tell you I know it. My voices have told me.' His voice was raised now and Toby felt his hand gripped so tight that it hurt. Behind him someone groaned and a bed-spring creaked. He turned and saw Swann lying on his back, his thumb firmly in his mouth.

'It's all right,' Hunter whispered, 'he's still asleep.' They could see Matron at the sink in the surgery, her back to them. Toby had to confess what was in his mind. He was doubting Christopher's honesty. He shouldn't be, he knew he shouldn't be, but he was.

'Matron told you, didn't she?' he said.

'Told us what?' Hunter said.

'About this afternoon, about what happened, down by the river, about the spears.'

'Has it happened already?' said Christopher, gripping his arm. 'Did they fight?'

'Well, no, not exactly.'

'Then what?' Hunter was leaning forward anxiously.

'Well it nearly happened. It would have if Matron hadn't been there.' And Toby went on to tell them the whole story, the scarecrow, Benjie's kidnap, the ambush, Porter's humiliation, everything. When he had finished neither of them spoke for a moment. He turned to Hunter.

'And you've been up here all afternoon, you sure?' he asked.

'Since lunch,' Hunter said.

'But the spears,' Toby said, 'how come you knew about the spears?'

'I told you,' Christopher sighed and smiled sadly. 'Why can't you believe me? My voices told me. Jesus told me. He never lies to me, Toby, he never has. You still don't believe in me, do you?'

'Yes, yes I do,' Toby insisted, ashamed of himself. 'I believe you, honestly I do.' And he did now, he truly did.

'You two,' Matron called from the door of the sick room – she had Custer by the collar. 'That'll be enough. Christopher needs his rest. Come along now, the tea-bell's gone.'

So they left Christopher reading his Bible. They both noticed that Swann was awake now. He followed them with his big eyes as they passed by the end of his bed.

'Do you think he heard us?' Hunter asked.

'Couldn't have,' said Toby. 'And even if he had he wouldn't have understood.'

'I'm not sure I do,' Hunter said as they walked along the corridor towards the stairs. 'I still don't know why I believe him. I haven't got any proof, none; but just after he fainted when he sat up and told me he'd just seen Jesus, that he was the Son of God, that he was Jesus come back again, I just believed him. I don't know why. You know what he said? He said if you believe then you don't need proof, and if you don't believe then proof won't make any difference.'

Toby was still trying to work that out when Mr Birley came rushing along the corridor towards them. As he came closer they could see there were tears in his eyes.

'Matron in?' His voice was choked.

'Yes, sir,' said Hunter, and then when he'd gone past, 'what's up with him?'

The second tea-bell was ringing downstairs. If you weren't there by the time it stopped ringing you missed your sticky bun. They took the stairs in twos and just made it.

Between tea and supper the talk was all of the latest skirmish with the 'oiks' down by the river. Porter, Runcy and Simpson between them had succeeded in whipping up violent anti-oik sentiment and were perplexed and clearly annoyed by Hunter's lack of interest and support. They had expected better of him. They protested noisily at Matron's intervention. At supper Simpson was still at it. 'Silly cow,' he said. 'All her fault. If she hadn't stuck her great big conk in we'd have had them, we'd have had the lot of them.' And then he retold the story of the de-bagging of Benjie and everyone was cock-a-hoop yet again. 'Anything they can do, we can do better,' he went on. Toby had said nothing throughout – it would be more than his life was worth to speak out, so strong was the feeling around the table. Simpson caught his eye.

'What's the matter, Jinks?' he said. 'Frightened of them are you? A bit yellow?'

'No,' said Toby quietly but he said no more and busied himself with his jelly and custard. He hated himself. He knew he should have stood his ground and said his piece, but he couldn't. Christopher would have done. Christopher wouldn't have hidden behind his face and said nothing. Simpson scoffed.

'Look at him,' he was saying, 'he's going to blub in his jelly,' and Toby felt a fierce anger welling inside him. He would tell them. He would tell them all that it was wrong. To do what they had done to Benjie was wrong. He took a deep breath and at last found the courage he needed. He looked up, but then he saw that Simpson wasn't talking about him, he wasn't talking about him at all. Everyone was peering towards the end of the table. Mr Birley sat gazing into space, his eyes vacant and watery. They were nudging each other and giggling surreptitiously. Mr Birley looked down at his jelly and sighed.

He pushed the bowl away from him and got to his feet. 'Excuse me,' he said, and he turned and left the dining-hall, almost colliding with Wanda as she backed in through the door pulling the trolley. As she turned the trolley and wheeled it up towards the High Table, Toby waited for her smile, but she never even looked in his direction. He ignored Simpson's barbed ridicule about 'Jinks's bit of stuff, Jinks's heart-throb' and kept his eye on her as she collected the dishes from Madame Lafayette's table. She tossed her hair back out of her eyes as she stood up from behind the trolley and then their eyes met at last. Toby had to look away. He could not endure her cold anger, her sudden disdain. She hated him. She blamed him for what had happened. He hadn't even been there and yet she blamed him. All through grace he had only one thought in his mind. He had to tell her he was not responsible for what had happened to Benjie. It wasn't his fault. She had to know.

It was his table's turn for changing-room duty. One table did it every evening after supper and before prep. They mopped down the wash-room, hung up any games clothes lying around on the changing-room floor and swept it from end to end. They weren't allowed to go until the duty master had inspected it. Toby knew Major Bagley would pass it, he always did; but he would be slow, horribly slow. And so it proved. By the time he reached the kitchen half an hour later Wanda had already gone. He had to be in prep in five minutes. He'd be late but didn't mind. He had to find her. He raced out across the playing-fields to see if he could catch her before she reached the road. A flock of starlings lifted off the rugby pitch and became a dark swirling cloud before settling in the treetops beyond the tennis courts, their thunderous chattering filling the evening air. There was no sign of Wanda. He ran on towards the field gate, climbed over and jumped down into the road. Wanda was walking towards the village, pulling up the collar of her coat. Toby called after her. She turned, saw him and then walked on even faster. Toby went after her. 'Wait Wanda, wait, please wait.' She stopped then and let him catch up with her. For some moments he was too breathless to gather his thoughts, let alone speak.

'You're just like the rest of them, aren't you?' He had never seen her angry like this. 'It's what Benjie said all along. He told me and he was right. I didn't believe him. I thought you were different, you know that. And I was wrong. What you done to him . . .'

'But I didn't! Honest, Wanda, I didn't do anything. I wasn't there.'

'What are you lying for? Benjie told me. He said you was there, in the fishing-hut. He told me. He told me everything. He ain't told Mum though, and you know why? Because he's got plans of his own and he don't want her getting in the way. He's going to sort you out, you and your poxy toffee-nosed school. And I'll tell you something else for nothing, when he does I'll be laughing, you hear me, laughing.'

'Please, Wanda,' said Toby, the words spilling out of him, 'Christopher and Hunter and me, we're going to stop it. I promise you we are. They shouldn't have done what they did to Benjie. It's not us, it's just Porter and his lot – but we'll stop them, honest we will. Christopher – he can do anything, you'll see, anything. He's got powers, honest he has, real powers.' And then he stopped. He'd said too much.

'Powers, what do you mean "powers"?' Toby yearned to tell her the truth, the whole truth, but he knew he couldn't. He'd promised, he'd sworn. And besides, she'd only laugh at him anyway, so he backtracked as best he could.

'He's . . . clever that's all. He'll tell them, persuade them, I promise he will. He'll stop it, I promise on the Holy Bible. I swear.'

For a moment Wanda seemed to believe him. Then she shook her head. 'It's what I hate about you people. You got the gift of the gab. You got all the words, you know how to string them together, you know how to spell them, but you don't know what they mean do you? You said you loved me, didn't you? Well you couldn't have, 'cos if you did you wouldn't have let that happen to Benjie. What he done to you – that was a mistake.

What you done to him, that was meant, planned that was. So don't you come around me no more with your fancy words, you hear me?' Every word she spoke was a knife in Toby's heart, draining him, numbing him. He saw Benjie coming along the road towards them on his motor-bike and he knew he had every reason to be frightened, but he was not. Benjie turned the engine off.

'He bothering you is he?'

'Leave him be, Benjie.'

'Hey, you ain't told him nothing, have you?' Benjie said.

'Course not.'

'Cos you know what, Toff, you lot down the school, you got a bit of a surprise coming your way after what you done. You sure you ain't said nothing, Wanda?' Wanda was walking round the side of the bike.

'What would I tell him for?' she said.

'You were sweet on him, weren't you?'

'Yes,' said Wanda, looking straight at Toby as she swung her leg over the bike and sat down behind Benjie, her hands on his shoulders. 'Yes, I was sweet on him, but I ain't any longer.'

Benjie smiled at him, a smile of pure venom, kicked the engine into life and roared off. As the bike leaned into the bend in the road and disappeared, Toby felt his soul melting away. He was just a body standing in the road and it was beginning to rain.

CHAPTER 7

WIDE-EYED AND UNSEEING, TOBY MOVED ACROSS the playing-fields like a sleepwalker. The windblown crows cackled darkly as they flew home to the high elms behind the pavilion and the cold whipped through his shirt and chilled him. He heard himself sobbing and wondered how that could be because there was nothing in him but emptiness. He was beyond misery.

Someone had left a solitary rugby ball on the pitch. It was something to do so he walked over to it and kicked at it. The ball skewed off, caught the wind and flew into the rhododendrons in front of Mr Birley's house. Toby thrust his hands into his pockets and thought about the detention that he knew was waiting for him when he got back. He was already late for prep, very late now, and if he was very late, then he might as well take his time. In

hard about. If there is a God, and I doubt it, I really doubt it, then he's a monster. He's a cruel, unfeeling monster.'

'Don't say that, you mustn't. And don't cry so, she'll hear you. You know how it upsets her.'

'Well, she won't be hearing me for long, will she?' he said bitterly.

'I haven't given up hope, my darling, and you mustn't either. I won't let you.'

'For God's sake. You heard what the doctor said.' Mrs Birley stroked his hands and kissed them.

'Doctors have been wrong before.' She spoke so softly that Toby could hardly hear. He crept a little closer and a twig cracked loudly beneath his foot. He crouched low. Both of them were looking in his direction now. Mr Birley got up off the swing and was coming towards him. 'Who is it? Who's in there?'

Toby thought of running but he knew he'd be seen. He'd have to brave it out as best he could. 'Me, sir,' he said, emerging from the bushes. 'I was just collecting a ball. I kicked it, sir.'

'Jenkins, isn't it? You should be in prep. Come over here.' As soon as he was near enough Mr Birley took Toby roughly by the arm and pulled him closer. 'You've been listening, haven't you, eavesdropping?'

'I didn't mean to, sir, honest. Honest I didn't, sir, I didn't mean it.'

'He's telling the truth, Arnold,' Mrs Birley intervened.

'You can see he is. Let him go. Let him go.' The grip on his arm relaxed.

'I'm sorry, Jenkins,' Mr Birley said, and he turned away. 'I'm sorry.'

'You heard? About Jenny?' Mrs Birley said as she drew Toby aside. 'Well, Mr Birley and me, we don't want anyone else to know, no one, you understand? People know she's ill, but they don't know how bad she is. It's private, and we want to keep it that way. You understand, don't you?'

'He understands,' said Mr Birley, 'he's the boy I was telling you about. He lost his grandmother, only last week wasn't it, Jenkins?'

'Oh, yes.' Mrs Birley was nodding. 'I remember now. You poor boy. I'm so sorry.'

'You'd better get back to school, Jenkins,' said Mr Birley. 'Go on, you'll get detention else.' He seemed composed now.

Toby spoke his thoughts quite involuntarily. 'Sir,' he said, 'sir, I think I know someone, someone who could help.' Toby couldn't stop himself now, even though he knew he should. He had to give them hope. 'He's a sort of healer. He's got sort of powers, I know he has.' They looked at each other and then at Toby.

'What do you mean, "powers"?' said Mr Birley. 'What do you mean?'

Toby had gathered his senses by now. He knew he'd

gone too far, said too much already. 'I can't tell you any more,' he stammered, backing away, 'not yet. I'll have to ask him, sir.'

'But who?' Mr Birley came after him. 'Who is it?' And he was still calling after him as Toby blundered through the rhododendrons and back out on to the playing-field. He dropped the ball and ran all the way back to school.

He was ten minutes late for prep. He told Major Bagley he'd been 'going down successful', not original but the best he could think up all breathless as he was and on the spur of the moment. 'Very successful, I should think,' said Major Bagley looking at him over his glasses, his eyebrows twitching with disbelief. 'You're lucky I'm not sending you to see Mr Stagg.'

'Yes, sir.'

'You'll stay in, Jenkins, and do half-an-hour's detention. Sit.'

Toby did not mind. Detention would give him time to think, time to pluck up the courage to tell Christopher what he'd said, what he'd done.

He found Christopher later sitting cross-legged on his sick-room bed playing chess with Benedict Swann, and had to wait until Christopher let him win and Swann had gone back to his bed and was out of earshot. Toby told him the whole story, trying to explain as best he could why he had blurted it out as he had and dreading Christopher's disapproval. When at last he did look up he found Christopher smiling back at him.

'At last,' he said. 'At last, it seems you do truly believe in me. I'll talk Matron into letting me out for a walk tomorrow – after lunch. She won't mind, not if I say I want to take Custer for a walk. But I want you to tell Hunter. In everything we do, I want us all to be together.'

Christopher said not a word as the three of them walked across the rugby pitch the next afternoon towards Mr Birley's house. Custer chased crows and starlings, barked at the wind and pounced on an unsuspecting crisp packet. When they went through the white wicket gate into Mr Birley's garden, Custer stayed outside and mauled his crisp packet.

The door opened as they came up the path. Mr Birley was in his shirt sleeves. He peered anxiously beyond them to see if anyone else was there.

'Which of you . . .?' he began, and then looking directly at Christopher, 'Are you the one?'

'Yes,' said Christopher.

'All right, you'd better come in then,' and Mr Birley ushered them in through the front door into a sitting-room almost filled with a grand piano that was covered with photographs in silver frames. Mrs Birley rose from her chair, a handkerchief clutched in her fingers. One glance was enough to tell that every one of the photographs was of a small girl from babyhood to infancy, in a pram, in Mrs Birley's arms, sitting on a beach with no clothes on waving a plastic spade, sitting astride a pony and smiling toothily.

'Now, Jenkins,' Mr Birley said, turning to face them in front of the fireplace, 'what's all this about? Mrs Birley and me, we . . .'

Christopher interrupted. 'May I see her?' he said. Mrs Birley stepped forward and looked at Christopher closely.

'You can heal?' she said. 'You can really heal?'

'Yes,' Christopher replied. 'Yes, I can.'

'I don't know that I like this,' said Mr Birley. 'Hocus-pocus, black magic, I've never liked this sort of thing.'

'Jesus was a healer,' she said, 'and there've been others since. I've heard about them. We must try, Arnold. You know that. We must try anything, and after all, it can't do any harm, can it?'

'And what are you doing here, Hunter?' Mr Birley sounded sharp, suspicious almost.

'He's a friend,' said Christopher. 'We're all friends.'

'All right,' said Mr Birley, his eyes flitting nervously. 'All right, but no one must know. You understand? If anyone finds out, if Mr Stagg . . .'

'He won't know. No one will ever know,' said Christopher, 'not unless you tell them.'

'She's in her room,' said Mrs Birley, 'upstairs. Shall I go with you?'

'I'll find it,' said Christopher, and he left the room. They heard him climbing the stairs and a door opening and closing. They sat in awkward silence, Hunter beside Toby on the sofa, Mrs Birley, her arms around her knees, twisting the handkerchief around her fingers and trying to smile at them. Mr Birley stood by the window looking out, his hand resting on a bronze sculpture of a sleeping deer. Toby thought of telling them something more about Christopher, to reassure them, but he thought better of it at once. There'd be questions, questions he couldn't answer if he was to maintain his vow of secrecy, and above all he had to do that. He kept quiet. A grandfather clock ticked loudly in the corner of the room and was hammering out three o'clock when they heard Christopher's voice upstairs and then a door shutting. Christopher came into the room, his face fatigued and pale. He nodded at Mrs Birley. 'It's all right,' he said. 'She'll get better.'

'You're sure?' said Mrs Birley, her hand to her mouth. 'You're quite sure?'

'Quite sure. She'll be fine. I promise.'

Toby and Hunter followed him out of the house, down the path to the playing-fields where Custer was still busy at his shredded crisp packet. He had to be dragged away from it.

'You didn't tell them who I was, did you?' Christopher asked as they walked away.

'No, course not,' said Toby, as if he hadn't even thought of it.

'No one must know, not yet, not until they're ready for it. Once they know they'll hate me, and if they hate me they will not listen to me later on when I'm older, when my work really begins. We must tell no one, no one.' And Toby shuddered inwardly when he remembered how close he had been to telling Wanda everything in the lane the day before. 'Let them know me as a healer if you want, as a peacemaker – that will do for the moment.'

'But I don't understand,' said Hunter. 'How can you know, how can you be so sure?' He was echoing Toby's own doubts. 'How can you really know she'll get better? I mean Toby said they'd just about given up hope, that the doctor said . . .'

Christopher sighed. 'You'll see,' he said. 'You'll see. I'm tired now. I think I'll take Custer back to Matron. Be sure you keep your eye on the river, and on Porter in particular, just in case.' He stroked Custer's head and smiled at them. 'He follows me without question, without doubts. You must learn to do the same.' And they both watched him walking away, Custer at his heels, and he didn't even have to call him.

They went to see Christopher in the sickroom each day after that and always found him with Benedict Swann, playing chess or just talking together. The two were becoming great friends. Toby felt that twinge of jealousy again and tried to hide it from Christopher. He wondered whether Swann would soon be joining their brotherhood. 'Have you told him?' he asked. 'About you, about us?'

'No,' said Christopher. 'He's too young, he wouldn't understand.' Toby was relieved at that.

Matron wouldn't let Christopher out again, even to walk Custer. 'There's a chill wind,' she said. 'He tires easily. He's not as strong as he looks.' And each time they left, Christopher would remind them about the river, to keep their eyes and ears open, but he said nothing more about Jenny.

Mr Birley seemed as distraught as ever and Toby dared not ask after Jenny. He and Hunter talked of her in hushed whispers, Hunter always the more confident, the more sure of Christopher. Toby sought to bolster his frail belief by testing Hunter's. 'She will get better, won't she?' Toby asked as they came away from visiting the sick room one afternoon.

'Course,' Hunter retorted. 'Course she will.'

The secret alliance, the growing bond between Hunter and Toby seemed to affect even their partnership on the rugby field. With Hetherington off-games again that week – an ear infection this time, another victim of the Tuesday run – they played together with an intuitive understanding that surprised and delighted Mr Price and everyone else who saw them. No signals seemed to be needed, no words. A glance between them, and Toby would seem to know what Hunter had in mind, whether he was going blind-side or open, whether he was dropping a goal. Passes flew long and straight from the base of the scrum and Hunter was always there on the end of them to pick them up. Toby revelled in the joy of it and basked in the admiration that came their way after each game.

He was in the changing-room that Saturday afternoon after a school match, a match they had won triumphantly. He was rubbing himself down after his bath. There was still some mud left on the back of his calf. He rubbed it off and sat back on the bench as he dried his chest and arms. He hadn't seen Wanda for several days now. He'd avoided her on purpose. He so much dreaded another look of rejection that he didn't want to risk it. He'd tried not to think of her. He'd tried very hard, but that moment in the lane kept coming back to haunt him.

'Gone off you, has she?' Porter laughed at him, flicking his towel at him as he sauntered past towards his locker. Toby paid him no attention – it was the best way. He was putting on his trousers seconds later when he felt a piece of paper in his pocket. It hadn't been there before. Puzzled, he took it out. The paper was folded several times and was as thin as a cigarette. He unfolded it, smoothed it out on his knee, and read it. 'DON'T GO DOWN THE PARK ON SUNDAY'. The writing was in scrawled capitals, in biro; and not signed. He looked around the changing-rooms to see if anyone had been watching him reading it, but no one had. He read it again. 'Down the park. Down the park'. Wanda, it had to be. No one else would write like that.

'Love letters is it now?' Porter scoffed from the far end of the changing-room, and Toby scrunched the paper up and thrust it deep into his pocket. He dressed quickly, scarcely hearing the hooting and jeering Porter was orchestrating.

Hunter spoke up for him with quiet authority. 'Porter,' he said, 'why don't you just shut up?' You could see that Porter thought for a moment about challenging Hunter. Toby could see it flash across his face, but he didn't. Instead, Porter turned to Runcy and Simpson, and they huddled together conspiratorially, whispering just loud enough to be heard but not loud enough to provoke.

Toby went to look for Wanda in the kitchen before supper. He had to know for sure that it was her who had sent the note, to find out what it meant. He'd thought of confiding in Hunter but he dared not. He'd spoken to no one of his love for her, not even Christopher, though he often suspected Christopher knew everything there was to know about him, a thought he found unnerving. He decided against it. There was no need to tell Hunter, not yet anyway. He pushed open the kitchen door. Mrs Woolland was not her usual friendly self. 'Shoo!' she said, waving him away. 'I can't have you boys wandering in and out of here like you own the place. There's work to be done – there's some people have to work for a living, you know that. Dinner for ninety doesn't make itself.' Toby made to speak as he backed away. She went on. 'And Wanda's not here, no. I've given her the weekend off. Now hop it.'

He had the piece of paper in his pocket all through chapel the next morning. He took it out and read it again and again during the sermon. It was still in his pocket when up went he and Hunter to see Christopher after letter-writing and still he hadn't made up his mind whether or not to go to the park that afternoon. He was alternately intrigued or alarmed. Something nasty was going to happen, that much he was sure of. Benjie was up to something, and he wanted to be there, he ought to be there to stop him. He couldn't warn anyone because if he did they'd ask him how he knew and then he'd have to tell them about Wanda. He couldn't do that. If he could only find some way to ask Christopher what he should do, without telling him about Wanda, then he would. He'd almost made up his mind to try, but Swann was there again, dejected, by his bed.

'Swann's being let out,' said Christopher. 'And

Matron says I should be out tomorrow if the doctor passes me.' He turned to Swann. 'Cheer up,' he said. 'They'll look after you, won't you?' And Swann did the best he could to smile. Christopher was still anxious about the river, about whether there was any trouble brewing. Hunter shook his head.

'All quiet on the western front,' he said. 'There's been rumblings, you know, the usual – Porter and Simpson telling everyone what they would do if they got the chance. But it's all talk.'

'Don't be so sure,' said Christopher. 'The flame has been lit. It needs only the oxygen of hate to fan it, and there's plenty of that.' He looked hard at them both and spoke earnestly, urgently. He leant forward. 'Be in the park this afternoon. Promise me you'll be there. I'd come myself but she won't let me out. Something's going to happen – I know it is. My voices have told me.'

'Do I have to leave?' Swann was pleading, tugging at Christopher's dressing gown.

'You'll be all right,' Christopher said, patting his arm. 'Just stick with these two. They'll look after you. They're my friends, my good friends.'

Toby's hand was on the paper in his pocket. This was the moment. He would tell them about the letter, about Wanda. He had only to speak.

'You two!' It was Matron calling from the surgery. 'You two, out of there, and you can take Swann with you. He's all mended, but he's off-games.'

The moment for the truth had passed. But at least one question was resolved, he would have to go to the park now because Christopher had told them to. There was no doubt in his mind about it now, something was going to happen in the park that afternoon. Wanda's letter had warned him and Christopher had prophesied.

The park was full of boys, as it always was on a Sunday afternoon if it was fine weather. A few people were kicking rugby balls about on the playing-fields, but almost everyone was messing around in the park – climbing trees, playing conkers, cow-pat fights, building camps; or, a favourite at this time of year, rolling down Woody Hill until your head whirled and it made you giddy. But unusually there were masters too in the park that afternoon. Rudolph had asked for volunteers to help him clean out the swimming-pool which had been emptying all that week. It was an annual ritual that no one relished one bit. Volunteers only volunteered because there would be a cream-tea laid on for them by Cruella afterwards as a reward. Cream-tea or no cream-tea it was not Toby's idea of fun. He'd done it before, scooping up the newts and frogs from the sludge at the bottom and emptying them out into the long grass beyond the swimming-pool fence. Then you had to scrub down the walls, Rudolph and Pricey hosing where you scrubbed. It took hours and you got very cold and Rudolph usually lost his temper when things weren't done quite as he wanted. Besides, Toby had other more important things on his mind, as did Hunter.

They decided to split up so that if and when trouble started one of them would be close by. Hunter went off towards the rhododendron chapel – he'd been going on about how it needed some clean straw on the floor and some tidying up. 'I can see all the way down to the river from there,' he said, 'and I'll do some repairs to the entrance while I'm there – don't want the cows getting in do we? Nor anyone else for that matter. I've pinched a bale of Mr Woolland's straw for the floor. The cows won't mind. Give us a shout if you see anything.'

Toby took Benedict Swann with him and went on down past the swimming-pool through the willow-copse and out into the water-meadows beyond – the only place Hunter couldn't see from the chapel. Benedict Swann was looking for molehills and chattering on about them. 'Christopher said that if you scoop away the molehills you'll always find a hole. Christopher said all you've got to do is put your ear to the hole and if you're lucky you can hear them digging and chewing worms. That's what Christopher said.' And he knelt down by a fresh molehill and scooped away the loose earth. Sure enough there was a hole. He put his ear to the ground and then looked up shaking his head in disappointment. 'Perhaps they're asleep,' he said. 'Come on, Jinks, let's try another.' They tried another, and another, and another. All over the water-meadows they tried and Toby found himself bullied into listening to every molehill between the swimming-pool and the dew-pond. Then, at last, Swann whooped with joy. He could hear something, he swore it. 'Cross my heart and hope to die. You listen, you listen.' But when Toby tried he couldn't hear a sound. He pretended he could though, to keep Swann happy. Now he'd pretended once, he had to pretend again and again, listening carefully each time and looking suitably surprised and delighted. It was an absorbing charade.

Time passed and all thoughts of trouble, of Christopher's warnings, vanished from Toby's mind. His back ached. He stood up and looked about him, stretching his back. The swifts chased each other screaming down the valley and a gang of rooks harried a pair of mewing buzzards. He followed the dog-fight until the sun dazzled his eyes and he had to look away. He looked around for Swann, but he was nowhere to be seen. The meadow was empty. As he looked about him, a shout went up from beyond the willow-copse, a fearful shouting that turned at once to screaming, a screaming that lifted the hair on the back of his neck. He ran through the willows ducking the low-slung branches, side-stepping the trunks, leaping fallen trees, and then he was out in the open. Rudolph was bellowing from inside the swimming-pool enclosure and dozens of boys were running towards him from all ends of the park, stumbling, tripping, some of them crying as they ran. Swann alone stood still, looking about him like a lost child. Pricey was bellowing at him from the swimming-pool fence, beckoning him frantically. Whatever it was that was terrifying them, Toby couldn't see it. Swann was rubbing his eyes with his knuckles and he was beginning to cry. Christopher's words rang in Toby's head: 'They'll look after you, they're my friends, they're my good friends.' He had to be near Swann to protect him, that was all he knew. Still the boys streamed down towards the swimming-pool enclosure, some pushing and shoving through the gate, others vaulting the fence, until every one of them was safe inside. They lined the fence now, screaming at Swann and pointing. And then Hunter came leaping down Woody Hill, shouting and gesticulating wildly, but he was too far away for Toby to hear what he was saying.

It was then that Toby saw what they had already seen. A bull came trotting into view from behind the swimming-pool hut, tossing his head and snorting, his ringed nose lifted in the air. A great brown bull he was, with long curved horns like a Viking's helmet. Swann stood not twenty paces from the bull. He had seen it too, but was frozen with fear. The bull came on now towards him, and behind came the cows cavorting, tails swishing.

A silence had fallen over the park as Swann at last began to back away. Toby could see he was thinking of running. 'Stay where you are!' he called. 'I'm coming. Don't move.' Everything in him told Toby to run, to leave Swann and run for it, instead he found himself walking slowly towards the bull. And as he did so he heard Christopher's voice speaking to him inside his head. 'You can do it. Do it for me. Do it for Swann.' And he felt suddenly cocooned, protected, wrapped in the velvet cloak of Christopher's calm.

The bull had seen him coming. He stopped, tossed his head and licked himself on the shoulder, his tongue whipping out and sending a shower of saliva along his back. And then he was still, his white eye fixed on Toby.

Rudolph's shout was a distant echo. 'Run boy, for God's sake run!' Toby ignored him. Out of the corner of his eye he sensed Hunter side-stepping down Woody Hill. He knew as he spoke that it was not his voice. It was Christopher speaking through him. 'I'm right behind you, Swann. Don't look round. We'll be all right. We'll be all right.' And then he was beside him, an arm around him, and Hunter was there too. 'You take him,' said Toby quietly, his eye on the bull's eye. But as he walked on alone he began to wonder why he wasn't frightened. He should be frightened. What if Christopher wasn't protecting him? The bull lifted his head and roared at him. A sudden terror tightened his stomach.

He stopped because his legs would not carry him any further. Why wasn't Christopher talking to him any more? Why had he deserted him? If the bull charged now he knew he would not be able to move. The bull snorted again and moved his head to one side to glare at Toby with his other eye. He bellowed again, lowered his head and began to paw at the grass. 'Oh, God,' Toby said, 'oh, Jesus.'

CHAPTER 8

THE BULL LICKED HIS NOSE, FIRST ONE NOSTRIL
and then the other, his tail swishing the face of the cow
behind him. Flies bunched in the corners of his eyes and
the skin on his neck twitched away a cluster of squatting
bluebottles. He blinked lazily and moved forward,
shifting his great weight from shoulder to shoulder. Toby
could smell his breath now, milky and sweet, he was that
close. When he reached out to touch him it was more to
protect himself than anything else, for his legs seemed
welded to the ground and still would not move. The hair
between the bull's eyes was coarse, close and curly. Toby
put the flat of his hand against his head and when the
bull began to rub up against it, it seemed the most
natural thing to scratch him back. It was what Custer
would have wanted. He seemed to like it. For several

moments he let Toby scratch him. Then he lifted his head and they touched noses momentarily. Toby felt the wet on his nose and wiped it away. 'Hello,' he whispered, surprised he could find a voice to speak with, and the bull eyed him again and turned his head away to consider the crowd beyond the swimming-pool fence.

The sound of a distant tractor engine broke the silence. Toby looked beyond the swimming-pool to the river below. The tractor did not slow as it splashed through the river and up into the park. The cows' heads turned but the bull ignored them and leaned against Toby's chest, rubbing his head up and down asking to be scratched again. Toby responded, holding one of the horns to keep his head still. The tractor roared and rattled its way up the hill, dipped out of sight behind the swimming-pool hut, circled the cows along the bottom of Woody Hill and stopped a few paces away. The cows set up a strident lowing that echoed around the park. Two people jumped off the tractor. The one with a rope in his hand and coming towards him slowly was Mr Woolland. He always wore the same battered sailor's hat on the side of his head and the same long dark coat tied around with binder cord. The other made to follow him. 'You stay where you are, Wanda, you hear me?' said Mr Woolland. Wanda was hardly recognisable with her hair tucked under her hat, but the look she gave Toby filled him with happiness. There was anxiety in her eyes, admiration, maybe even love.

'Now, young feller-me-lad,' Mr Woolland said, as he came towards him, 'you just scratch his head, he likes that does Big Tom. Don't do nothing sudden and we'll be right as rain the two of us. Soon as I come alongside you, you move away easy like and I'll get the rope on him. Wanda,' he called, 'soon as I've got him, throw out that hay from the link-box, it'll keep the cows happy whilst I take him home. Oo oo da boy, oo oo da boy. Easy now, easy now.' And then he was beside Toby and scratching the bull between his horns. 'You silly old codger,' he muttered. 'What're you doing going walk-abouts? Wanted to see your lady friends, eh? Bit lonely, that it?' And he slipped the rope through the bull's ring and took a deep breath. 'Silly beggar. Right, you can chuck that hay out now, Wanda. Come along now, Tom. I don't think Mr Stagg is going to be very pleased with us somehow.' And he led the bull over towards the swimming-pool fence. 'Sorry about that, sir.' Toby didn't think he sounded all that sorry. 'Some little blighter must've left the gate open. Don't you worry, sir, I'll have his guts and no mistake.' Mr Stagg was shaking his head, mopping his neck with his handkerchief.

'I tell you, Mr Woolland, it's not good enough. Not good enough at all. Someone could've been hurt, killed even.'

'I dare say you're right, sir, and like I say, I'm sorry. Like the poet says, eh, all's well that ends well. Isn't that.

what he said? No harm done. Won't happen again you can be sure of that. Brave lad of yours that, standing up to Big Tom. Took some nerve.'

'Yes,' said Mr Stagg, managing a smile now. 'He did a fine thing all right, but it's no more than I'd have expected of him.' Toby glowed at this unexpectedly fulsome praise. He felt everyone's eyes on him and loved it. He just wished he could stop trembling. Wanda was beside him, her hand on his arm.

'You all right, Little Toff?'

'I think so,' said Toby.

'Why'd you come?' she whispered. 'I told you, I warned you didn't I? You got my letter didn't you?'

Toby looked at her. 'Yes,' he said. And then, 'It was Benjie, wasn't it? He did this, didn't he?'

'I couldn't stop him. I tried, honest I did; but he wouldn't listen, and I couldn't tell on him, could I? I mean, he's my brother. But why didn't you stay away like I said?'

'I couldn't,' said Toby. 'Hunter and me, we had to come, to look after Swann, to keep an eye on the river. Christopher, he . . .' He'd stopped himself in time.

'He what?' she said.

'Nothing.'

'Well, I'll tell you something for nothing,' said Wanda, 'that Tom, he's a mean old devil. You was lucky, you was really lucky.'

'It wasn't luck,' Toby said.

'Come on, Wanda,' Mr Woolland called out. 'You take the tractor home. I'll take Tom,' and he spoke to Mr Stagg again. 'Anyways,' he was chuckling, 'you got yourself a real live bullfight, and a real live matador.' He turned to Toby. 'What's your name, son?'

'Toby Jenkins.'

'El Toby then,' he said, and his chuckling became a belly laugh. 'El Toby.' And he walked away leading Big Tom down the hill towards the river, Wanda driving behind him on the tractor and smiling back at Toby as she went. And then the boys were climbing over the fence and coming out through the gate and everyone was rushing towards him. Rudolph pumped his hand, Pricey clapped him on the back and he found himself surrounded and feted.

'Good lad,' said Rudolph beaming. 'I'm proud of you, proud of you.' Then he called for his cleaners again and reluctantly they followed Rudolph and Pricey back to the swimming-pool enclosure. Swann was suddenly there, smiling up at Toby and reaching for his hand, and everyone was cheering and chanting.

'We saw them, we saw them,' Porter was shouting at him over the hubbub. 'It was the oiks. They were watching on the other side of the river. They did it, the oiks did it.' And only then, as Porter punched his fist into the air, could Toby make out what they were all chanting.

'Down with the oiks! Down with the oiks! Down with the oiks!' Suddenly the sweet taste of triumph was soured. Toby felt sickened and used. They tried to hoist him on their shoulders, but he wouldn't have it. Enraged, he shouted to be let down. Ahead of him Hunter turned round, and came back, pushing through the crush to help him.

'What's the matter with you?' said Porter and the crowd silenced at once, sensing a confrontation.

'You just want to fight them, don't you?' said Hunter squaring up to him. 'You don't know how that bull got into the park, do you? You heard what Mr Woolland said, a gate was left open. All right, maybe it was on purpose; but maybe it wasn't, you haven't thought of that have you? And even if it was on purpose, no one got hurt. There's no harm done. I'm telling you, you've got to stop this before someone does get hurt. Let's call it quits. Let's forget it. We leave them alone, they leave us alone.'

Porter shook his head. 'I don't believe I'm hearing this. You've changed, you know that? What they did to Jinks the other day, that wasn't an accident. And that bull wasn't an accident either.' He turned away and raised his voice. 'It's a war, right?'

'Yes,' came the cry.

'Who do we hate?'

'Oiks, oiks, oiks, oiks, oiks, oiks!' The chanting was

unanimous. Hunter raised his hands to quell the chorus. Toby could see that he was desperate.

'All right, all right,' he said, 'but if you're going to declare war we've got to do it properly. A school meeting, here in the park, tomorrow evening; then we can all decide. And in the meantime no one does anything, no crossing the river, no shouting at them, no stones, nothing. That's fair, isn't it? Well, isn't it?' The quad bell was ringing out over the park. 'Agreed?' Hunter demanded, swinging around challenging them all until he faced Porter again. No one spoke up. 'Right then,' Hunter said. 'After prep tomorrow, and a truce until then.'

Toby felt very ambiguous about his triumphant reception at school. He was the conquering hero, the knight in shining armour. It should have been better than scoring the winning try in a school match, better even than having your grandmother die. He loved all the attention and the glory, but he knew in his heart of hearts that it had not been him at all facing the bull in the park, that it was Christopher who had made it all possible. Yet at the same time he liked to think that maybe he could have done it without him, and then again he knew that wasn't likely. He tried to soak in the teachers' smiles, the worshipping glances of the juniors, the adulation of all his friends. Even Custer seemed to sense he was the hero of the hour and followed him around and sat at his feet. He should have been able to bask in it all, but he couldn't.

Matron, of course, poured cold water on the whole thing. When they went to see Christopher that evening in the sick-room she looked him up and down and said in a heavily Spanish accent, 'Ah, El Toby. Matador extraordinaire. Come to have your wounds bound, have you?' And she danced a mock flamenco around the surgery. Toby wondered for a moment if she'd been drinking. 'Quite the little St Francis, aren't we?' It was nearer to the mark than she knew. 'In you go then, he's been asking for you,' she said.

Hunter told Christopher the whole thing, blow by blow, and Christopher nodded throughout rather as if he knew most of it already. Toby waited and then put the question he was burning to ask. 'It was you, wasn't it? You were there, weren't you, inside me, I mean?'

'If you want me,' said Christopher, 'I will always be with you, inside you.' Toby didn't like that in him. Sometimes he just would not answer a straight question. Hunter went on to tell him about the school-meeting in the park.

'I couldn't do anything else,' he explained. 'I tried, but I couldn't stop them. You have to speak to them. There'll be a war else and I won't be able to stop it. They'll listen to you, I know they will.'

Christopher sighed deeply. 'All right, I'll speak to

them,' and he turned back to Toby. 'Wanda was there then?' he said. 'So you're friends again?' So he did know, he'd known all along. Christopher leaned closer to him. 'The applause is for God, remember that Toby and enjoy it. You did well. You both did well.'

Christopher was allowed out of the sick-room the next morning after the doctor's visit and they met in the rhododendron chapel after lunch. Swann tagged along with them everywhere now. He might not be a fully fledged disciple, but Toby could see that Swann had become one of them now and undetachable. They knelt down in the clean straw in the rhododendron chapel and prayed together in silence, until Swann had to go and sit outside because the dust in the straw made him sneeze. 'Porter's the one you've got to persuade,' said Hunter, 'him and Runcy and Simpson. There's a whole bunch who'll follow them whatever they do.'

'Well, let's pray that God will speak to them through me, and that they will listen,' said Christopher. 'And Toby, when you next see Wanda, tell her we're all brothers and sisters under God. Get her to tell them that in war everyone loses and everyone suffers. Tell her we want peace. Tell her from me, and let's pray that she, too, will listen.'

Toby and Wanda found each other after supper and sat side by side on a bench behind the pavilion. 'No one will see us here,' said Wanda and she reached out and held his hand. Toby needed to get one thing settled in his mind, he had to be sure of her.

'What you said to me, you know, out in the lane, with Benjie, did you mean it?' Wanda laughed and that made him feel silly.

'Course not, you little Toff, I was just cross, wasn't I? Allowed to be cross, aren't I? What happened to Benjie, it wasn't your fault, I know that now.' Toby looked out over the valley, the shadow of those dreadful words at last obliterated. 'I love you, little Toff, you know that?'

'Me too,' said Toby, and she kissed him and put her head on his shoulder.

A tractor was parked by the hay barn on the far side of the river and Mr Woolland was knocking in some stakes. 'My dad,' Wanda said, 'he thinks you're something. Benjie does too. I told him what you done and he said you got to have plenty of bottle to do that.'

'What did he do it for?' Toby asked. 'I mean someone could have been really hurt.'

'He was mad, that's all, mad with the lot of you. Can't hardly blame him can you, not after what they done to him?' She passed her cigarette across to him. He shook his head. 'Don't really like them,' Toby said, risking being honest about it at last.

'You're funny,' Wanda said, smiling at him. 'Sometimes you're like a little kid, and then you're like a real man. I mean like yesterday in the park with Big Tom.

Cool as a cucumber you were, just stood there stroking him. No one's done that to Tom before, not even Dad. Benjie says he'd have run a mile. Weren't you frightened or anything?'

'Course I was,' Toby said, 'but . . .' He wasn't sure he should go on, but he did. 'But I wasn't on my own, not exactly.'

'What d'you mean?'

'You know Christopher – the one your lot threw stones at in the river – well, he sort of helped me.'

'How d'you mean, helped?'

He wanted to tell her. He would tell her. She would understand, he was sure of it. She wouldn't laugh at him. He could trust her. He wouldn't tell her everything, not everything – he couldn't do that. 'Well, it's like he spoke to me in my head. Like he was there telling me what to do and I just did it, that's all. He was sort of taking me over from the inside.'

'That's crazy.'

'No it's not. It's like he was a spirit, the Holy Spirit. And he can heal too, he's got powers, honest he has. He can see inside me, he can see inside everyone and he can tell what's going to happen – well, sometimes he can. He hears these voices and they tell him.'

'What voices? What're you on about?' There was disbelief in her voice, a hint of mockery.

'Doesn't matter,' Toby said, and he got up suddenly

and walked away. She came after him and turned him towards her.

'Here, I didn't mean anything.'

'Yes you did,' said Toby. 'You don't believe me do you? I thought I could tell you. I thought you'd understand.' Toby felt his eyes filling with tears in spite of himself. 'He just wants good things to happen. It's him that's trying to stop this war. He says we're all brothers and sisters. It doesn't matter where we come from, how we speak, none of that. He wants peace. He told me to tell you, and we've got to pray for it, else nothing will come right.'

'I don't believe in all that stuff, not since Sunday school anyway.'

'I didn't think I did either,' said Toby, 'not really. I just did it, y'know like a sort of habit. But it's different now.'

'Why, what's different?'

'Because of him, because of Christopher.' Toby lowered his voice now, almost afraid to hear himself. 'I can't tell you any more. It's a secret. I said I wouldn't tell anyone. I promised.' But he knew already he was going to tell her.

'Come on,' she said. 'I won't tell anyone, honest I won't. Cross my heart. Oh go on. I love you remember? You can tell me, you can trust me.'

'You promise, promise faithfully?'

'Course I do.' And Toby looked at her and believed her.

'He's Jesus,' he said. 'Christopher, he's Jesus come back again, like it said he would in the Bible. Christopher is Jesus. It's true. There's nothing he can't do, nothing. I know it sounds mad but you should see the things he does, hear the things he says. He is Jesus, I know he is, that's all.' And he told her everything, everything that had happened since Christopher's vision in the rhododendron chapel, about Hunter, about little Benedict Swann, about Mr Birley's dying daughter. When he'd finished she looked at him for a moment and then went and sat down on the bench.

'That little girl,' she said after a while. 'You think she'll get better, you really think so?'

'Course,' Toby said. 'You'll see. Christopher said so, he promised.'

Wanda lapsed into a long silence after that, her brow furrowed with thought. A little later they shared some cake she had purloined from the kitchen. She licked her fingers noisily and wiped them on her handkerchief. 'So you're like a kind of disciple, a follower, you and Hunter and Swann?'

'No, not Swann, he's too young.'

'And no one else knows?'

'Only you,' said Toby. 'You won't tell, will you? You won't ever tell? If he knew I'd told you . . .'

She shook her head. 'I won't say a word, not ever. I've got to go,' she said suddenly and she leant over and kissed him. 'I'm helping Dad with the milking. See you.' And she was gone round the corner of the pavilion. Toby followed her. She was already half way across the rugby pitch.

'You won't tell!' Toby called after her. 'You won't tell, will you?' She waved her hand over her head and ran on.

Toby heard a cheer go up from the park below. The meeting had started. He vaulted the iron railing below the rugby pitch and ran on down into the park. Woody Hill had become an amphitheatre, the grassy ledges the seats. From a distance it seemed as if the hillside had turned blue. Every boy in the school must be there, Toby thought. He saw Swann and Christopher and Hunter sitting together near the front. Porter was on his feet, railing; and whenever he paused for breath they cheered him wildly.

'He tried to make peace with them once before remember? And what did they do, they stoned him, didn't they? No, there's only one way with their sort.' He held his fist up in the air. 'This, this is all they under-stand. We've got to teach them. They've got to learn once and for all that they can't come waltzing over here just when they feel like it. This is our place and we don't want them here, do we? We let them get away with what they did yesterday and they'll be back again and again. And don't let him tell you yesterday was an accident.

They let that bull out on purpose, I know they did, you know they did. I say, let's do them, and properly, so's they never forget it.'

Toby sat down beside Hunter as they applauded yet again. Porter walked away gripping his hands above his head and conducting their cheers. Simpson clapped him on the back as he sat down. And then Christopher stood up and everyone fell suddenly silent.

'Porter is right,' he said, his voice so quiet you had to strain to listen. 'Porter says we have to teach them, and he's right. But what shall we teach them? Shall we teach them to throw more stones? Shall we teach them to make more scarecrows? Shall we teach them to throw more spears? Shall we?'

'Yes!' Simpson shouted, and he wasn't alone.

Christopher waited till they'd finished laughing. 'All right then, go ahead,' he went on. 'Throw your spears. Bit of luck you could put someone's eye out. Go ahead, throw your stones. Bit of luck you could even kill someone. Be one oik less, wouldn't it?' His eyes swept the meeting, challenging them to heckle. 'Of course, on the other hand they could get lucky. One of us could have his eye put out. One of us could be killed. It could be you, or you, or you, or even you.' He was pointing at Porter now. Porter tried to laugh it off but it was not convincing. Runcy and Simpson looked at each other nervously. Christopher hadn't finished. 'Yes, Porter was right. They have to learn, he said; and he's right, they do have to learn. But so do we. They have to learn to share this river and we have to learn to share this river. It's as much ours as theirs, and as much theirs as ours. So we must share it. All we have to do is put down our stones and they'll put down theirs. We throw away our spears, they'll throw away theirs. We stop hating them, they'll stop hating us. It's simple. One of us has to offer a hand of friendship across the river. One gesture of goodwill, that's all it'll take and this war will be over with. And if we can do it here in this place, if we can make a peace between us then it can be done everywhere and there'll be no more war, no more hate.'

'No more war!' cried Swann leaping to his feet. 'No more hate!' And then there were others on their feet and chanting. 'No, no, no more war! No, no, no more hate!' Porter, Runcy and Simpson were looking about them in bewildered disbelief. Within moments they were the only three still left sitting. The chanting spread like fire across the hillside, fists punching the air in unison. Toby found himself looking across at Christopher, who stood quite unmoved, his eyes closed. Toby knew he would be praying. He prayed too, just for a few moments. He prayed that Wanda would tell no one, that somehow Christopher would never find out what he had done.

When he opened his eyes Porter was barging his way up the hill, turning round to shout every few paces, but his words were drowned out and they were jeering at him before he reached the top of the hill. Simpson and Runcy ran after him and the three of them vanished into the trees. Hunter was beside Christopher now, holding up his hands for silence. It was some time before he could quieten them.

'All right then,' he said, 'from now on no one goes across the river. No more name-calling. No more sticks, no more stones. The war is over, over for good.' And the meeting broke up in a cacophony of clapping, cheering and chanting, with Swann holding Christopher's hand and dancing around him in wild excitement.

It was comforting for Toby to have Christopher back in the next bed that night. Christopher lay there in the moonlight, his hands behind his head, staring up at the shadows on the ceiling. Toby bashed his pillow into shape and turned over to talk to him. 'Can't you sleep either?' he whispered.

'Toby,' said Christopher, without looking at him. 'Toby, you wouldn't ever betray me would you?'

'Course not,' said Toby, and the moonlight moved across his face and lit his guilt. He looked away to hide it. 'Course not, what did you say that for?'

'Tomorrow night,' Christopher went on, 'tomorrow night I may not be here.'

'What do you mean?'

'I may be gone.'

'Gone where?'

'Home,' he said, 'where I belong. And you and Hunter will be alone. You've got to promise me you'll keep the faith. Promise me.'

'Why? What's going to happen?'

'Promise,' his voice was suddenly urgent, insistent, almost angry.

'All right, I promise,' said Toby.

'And tell Hunter for me. I may not have a chance in the morning. There may not be time tomorrow to say goodbye. I want you to look after Swann for me too, and keep your eye on Porter and his crowd. Whatever you do, keep your eye on Porter. He hasn't given up. He will do all he can to break the peace. And Toby, one last thing, thanks, thanks for believing. You were the first one and I'll always remember that.'

Toby propped himself up on his elbow. 'What're you saying all this for? What's going to . . .?'

The dormitory door opened suddenly and Rudolph stood framed in the corridor light. Toby froze where he was, hoping against hope Rudolph would not turn the light on. Their end of The Pit was the furthest from the door, the darkest. 'If I have to come in again it'll be the slipper for the lot of you, do you hear me?'

'Yes, sir,' came the mumbled chorus, and the door shut, plunging the dormitory into blackness. Toby breathed again.

'Go to sleep,' said Christopher. 'It's all right. It'll be all right.'

But Toby could not sleep. Christopher's words tumbled in his head and would not let him sleep. The quad bell struck every hour of the night. By six o'clock he still had made no more sense of it. Beside him Christopher slept, his breath shallow and even, his hands folded over his stomach. He even looks like a god, Toby thought, it's how a god would sleep.

It was not until breakfast that Toby began to think that something was up. Mr Birley came in late with Rudolph who strode purposefully to the High Table and rang the gong. He often did that if there was too much noise, but this was different – you could tell from the frown on his face. 'In the hall, everyone, right after this.'

Matron spoke up from the far end of the dining-room. 'But Mr Stagg, what about my surgery?'

'In the circumstances, Matron,' said Rudolph, 'your surgery will have to wait a while this morning.' He was stiff but polite. 'I won't keep you long.' For a moment Toby thought Matron would walk out. No one spoke to Matron like that, not even Rudolph. 'Carry on talking,' he said and sat down. But everyone was stunned into silence and no one talked. At the end of the table Mr Birley looked up and Toby saw then that his eyes were red with crying. Jenny's dead. Toby knew it at once and looked across at Christopher. But she couldn't have died,

Christopher had healed her. Christopher had promised. No, Jenny can't be dead, not if Christopher is Jesus like he says he is. But what if he's been lying all this time? What if the whole thing's been a hoax, a tease? Stop it, stop thinking that. Christopher is Jesus, he is, he must be, and if he is then Jenny's not dead, she can't be. Christopher scraped the last of the porridge off his bowl and reached for his tea. Toby tried to catch his eye but couldn't. He looked at Mr Birley again and found Mr Birley staring down the table at Christopher. There was despair in that look – but there was more than despair, there was hate too. Behind him Wanda came in with the trolley and began to hand out the dishes of bacon and fried bread. When she smiled at him, she smiled nervously and her eyes flitted over him to Christopher beyond. For a moment she paused, looked at him, and then she was hurrying away towards the High Table.

The bacon was cold and congealing, as it usually was. Toby did what he always did and spread marmalade all over it so he could forget the bacon underneath. When he'd finished he found Mr Birley still staring at Christopher who was gazing out of the window at a thrush hammering a snail on the window-ledge outside, beady-eyed and pleased with itself.

There was a hum of anticipation in the hall, silenced immediately by the sight of the study door opening and

Rudolph and the staff filing down the Bloody Steps and up on to the platform. Everyone stood up and then Rudolph began.

'Sit,' he said, hitching his gown higher up on his shoulders. 'Sit.' Every teacher was grim-faced. They were all there, Mr Birley, Pricey, Major Bagley, Mr Cramer, Madame Lafayette, even Holy Jo. Holy Jo shouldn't have been there. He only came on Tuesdays and Fridays. Matron was there, too, and Miss Whitland. Major Bagley was cleaning his glasses and shaking his head. Beside him sat Mr Birley, eyes cast up to the ceiling and full of tears. 'I have some bad news,' Rudolph began. 'I have some very bad news.'

CHAPTER 9

'YESTERDAY EVENING SOMEONE CAME TO SEE ME,' Rudolph went on. 'He was upset, very upset. He had never before come to me and complained about anything, never in all the long years he has been working here at Redlands. But this, he thought, was so serious and so horribly offensive that he could not let it pass. It seems we have amongst us a boy who claims he is Jesus Christ, that's right, Jesus Christ. This boy pretends he can heal, that he hears voices, that he is Jesus Christ come back to earth.' Toby tried to believe he wasn't hearing this, that it wasn't happening. 'I didn't believe him, not at first, I wouldn't have believed such a thing of any of my boys.'

As the first shock wore off, the implications of what Rudolph was saying became horribly clear to Toby. Christopher would know now for sure who had betrayed him, and he was sitting there right next to him. Toby stared down at the parquet floor unable to lift his head. He could not face the hurt in Christopher's eyes. He would never be able to face Hunter again. He had betrayed them just as surely as Wanda had betrayed him. But why had she done it? Who had she told?

Rudolph's voice lifted in anger. 'I told him as much. "Not possible" I said, "just a silly story" – that's what I hoped, that's what I believed. But I was able to check the story with another member of my staff, Mr Birley; and he confirmed enough of what I had been told. We have amongst us a blasphemer, a trickster, a con-man, a liar. Such people, once found out, are always cowards so I am quite sure he will not own up to his crime. But we shall see. Would the boy who claims he is the Son of God stand up?'

Christopher stood up at once. Toby glanced at him quickly. Christopher was serene. Every face in the hall was turned towards him. Rudolph seemed taken aback for a moment. 'Come up here, Christopher. Come up here where everyone can see you.' Christopher put his hand on Toby's shoulder as he moved past him. Toby saw forgiveness in his eyes, and understanding. Then he was up on the platform and standing in front of Rudolph. 'It was you then?' Rudolph asked, his fingers twitching on his gown. 'You're the one, you're the new Jesus, are you, the Son of God?'

'Your words, sir, not mine,' Christopher spoke just loud enough for everyone to hear.

Rudolph's temper snapped. 'You can stand there in front of the whole school and blaspheme like that. Do you know what you are saying? Do you?'

'Yes, sir.'

'Very well, very well. We'll put this to the test. Just so that everyone here will know what a liar you are, what a cheat you are. You went to see Mr Birley, am I right?'

'Yes, sir.'

'Mr Birley's daughter, Jenny, has been sick, bed-ridden, for the past two years or more, and you claimed you could heal her. You tried to heal her. You said she'd get better. Am I right?'

'Yes, sir.'

'That was almost two weeks ago, wasn't it?'

'Yes, sir.'

'Well, I want everyone here to know that unfortunately Mr Birley's daughter is just as ill as she was, if anything she is worse. You raised Mr and Mrs Birley's hopes falsely and that was cruel, cruel beyond words.' He paused. 'Not in all my ten years at Redlands have I ever expelled a boy; but then in all my ten years I have never known a boy as evil, as wicked, as you. In all my ten years I have never been so angry as I am now. I am not a vindictive man so I will give you a chance to redeem yourself. You will be punished of course, you would

172

expect that; but I will give you just this one chance to save yourself the disgrace, the ignominy of expulsion. If you will renounce now your ridiculous blasphemous claim to be Jesus Christ, if you will declare aloud for everyone to hear that it was no more than a childish trick then you may stay on here at Redlands. We will try to forgive, we will try to forget.' Christopher said nothing. 'Well, what do you say?'

'It's my voices who tell me who I am, sir, and my voices are real. I have not dreamt them, I have not made them up. They say I am Jesus and I believe them.'

'Do you know, Christopher, do you know what you are saying? Do you realise that if you'd said that just a few hundred years ago they'd have burnt you at the stake?'

'Yes, sir,' said Christopher, 'and a few hundred years before that they'd have crucified me.'

For several long moments Toby could see Rudolph trying to control himself, his mouth contorting, his fingers clutching his gown. The staff alongside him glanced at him anxiously and Holy Jo crossed himself and closed his eyes. 'Very well,' said Rudolph clearing his throat, 'you leave me no choice. Since you refuse to recant you will leave this school today. I shall telephone your home to that effect.' Christopher turned to leave the platform. 'Stay where you are, I have not yet finished.' Rudolph was seething. 'I am told you have followers, that you have infected at least two other boys with your dreadful blasphemy.' Toby's heart pounded in his ears. Rudolph was looking straight at him. There would be no point in denying it, yet he could not bring himself to confess, not in front of everyone. He'd follow Hunter. He'd wait for Hunter to own up. But beside him Hunter never moved and Toby dared not risk a sideways glance. 'I will not allow you to leave your poison behind you when you leave. I will put a stop to it now, once and for all. You see, I know who those two boys are. They have been foolish, not evil, not wicked like you. They have been duped. But they are implicated in your blasphemy. They have encouraged you, and for all I know helped to spread your lies. They too will have to be punished. Better for them if they own up to it now.' Toby could picture in that moment the look on his father's face, he could hear his anguished voice ringing in his ears. 'Expelled! Expelled! You have let yourself down, Toby. You have disgraced this family.' And he could see the disappointment and pain on his mother's face. 'I want the two boys concerned to stand up and show themselves.' Up near the front of the hall with the juniors, Swann was on his feet, his hand in the air.

'Me, sir,' he piped. 'It was me. I'm Christopher's friend, I'm his follower.' Rudolph frowned down at him and looked across at Mr Birley who shook his head.

'Sit down, Swann.'

'But, sir, I am, sir. Honest I am.' There were tears in his eyes. 'He's my friend, you can't expel him, you can't.'

Rudolph snapped angrily. 'That's enough, Swann, that's quite enough. I told you already, I know who the two boys are and you are not one of them. I just want to see if they are honest enough to admit it.'

Swann looked around the hall until his eyes settled on Toby and Hunter. He didn't point at them but it was as good as. Toby and Hunter rose together to face their shame. 'Up here,' said Rudolph. The walk up on to the platform seemed to last a lifetime. There wasn't a cough or a whisper in the hall. 'Well,' said Rudolph, 'and what do you have to say for yourselves? Not much, eh?' Toby stood next to Christopher hanging his head. 'I'm surprised at you both and disappointed, particularly with you, Hunter. To have to speak like this to the Captain of School – I would never have expected such a thing of you, never; and you, Jenkins, after what you did yesterday. I just can't think what came over you both. You're both intelligent. How could you be so gullible, so stupid as to listen to these terrible lies?' At this point Holy Jo intervened tremulously, his finger wagging.

'Remember what it says in the Bible. "Beware of false prophets". And in the Ten Commandments – "thou shalt not take the name of the Lord thy God in vain". That is what you have done.'

Rudolph was thrown momentarily by this

interruption, unsure as to whether Holy Jo had finished. 'Indeed,' he said at last. 'Indeed. But I want to be fair. As with Christopher I will give you one chance to redeem yourselves. If you do not recant, if you do not admit openly to everyone in this hall that this boy is just a boy like yourselves and nothing more, then like him you will be expelled. You, like him, will be home by tonight. Do I make myself crystal clear? Do I?'

'Yes, sir,' said Hunter, barely audible.

'Yes, sir,' said Toby.

'Well, is Christopher the Son of God? Is he Jesus?'

'We thought, sir . . .' Hunter began.

'Yes or no?' Rudolph cut him off sharply. 'Yes or no? No buts, no ifs. Yes or no? Do you or do you not believe that this boy standing beside you is Jesus the Son of God?'

Toby was suddenly sorely tempted. If he said yes he could be home by supper-time. He'd be back in his own bed. He'd never have to wake up to Latin tests, history tests or the Tuesday run ever again. He'd never have to dread the next morning. He'd never have to bend over Rudolph's leather chair in the study, never have to walk up the Bloody Steps; and besides, he did believe in Christopher, he'd only be telling the truth. If he said yes he'd be keeping the faith, he'd be standing by him. It would be the honourable thing to do, the right thing. He would be like Sydney Carton on the scaffold in *A Tale of*

Two Cities – 'it is a far, far better thing that I do, than I have ever done'. But then the doubts came flooding in. Jenny was still sick, Rudolph had said as much. Christopher had promised she'd get better and she hadn't, so maybe he wasn't who he said he was after all. And then there was his mother, her voice plaintive in his head. 'How could you do this to us, Toby? How could you, and so soon after Gran's death?'

'Well,' said Rudolph, 'I'm waiting.'

'No, sir,' said Hunter quietly.

'Louder,' Rudolph pounced triumphantly.

'No, sir.'

'You do not believe Christopher is the Son of God?'

'No, sir.'

'And you, Jenkins, what about you?'

'No, sir.'

'I want them to hear it at the back of the hall, Jenkins. "Christopher is not Jesus". Say it.'

'Christopher is not Jesus.' Toby said it out loud, but did not lift his head. He felt Christopher touch his arm.

'It's all right,' he said, 'it's all right.'

'Christopher,' said Rudolph, puffed up now with self-satisfaction, 'You will go to your dormitory and pack your trunk. Matron, will you see to it please?' Matron did not move but stared stonily at Rudolph. 'If you please, Matron,' said Rudolph.

'Come along, Christopher, I don't think you belong

here,' said Matron, and then under her breath as she passed them by, 'any more than I do.' As they walked away Christopher never once looked round and Toby was glad of that. Christopher might have forgiven him but he would never forgive himself for what he had done, never.

Once they had gone Rudolph turned to them again. 'And you two, I'll see you in my study now,' and he swept past them off the platform. They followed him past the rows of staring boys and up the Bloody Steps. 'I'll have you first, Hunter,' he said, and Hunter followed him into the study and the door shut behind them. Toby sat down on the settle and waited, his hands rubbing up and down on his knees, watching the boat rocking on the grandfather clock. It was ten past nine. By quarter past it would all be over, but he had those five minutes to live through. He felt sick to his stomach, and he needed to go to the lavatory. Cruella came out of the drawing-room and walked past him without so much as a glance, and Toby remembered the last time he'd been there and how kind she had been to him then. The cane swished once, twice, three times, and Cruella stopped and turned at the top of the steps.

'He doesn't mean it, you know. He doesn't enjoy it. It's for your own good.' And then, 'It'll soon be over with.' And she was gone.

The study door opened, and Hunter emerged, his face

red, his eyes full of pain. He was breathing hard as he paused by Toby and tried to smile. 'Good luck,' he said. 'What I said up there in front of everyone, I didn't mean it. I just couldn't . . . Well, you know.'

'I know,' said Toby, and full of new-found courage he strode into the study. The stag's head stared down at him from the wall. The severed elephant's foot was waiting for him.

Rudolph tapped the arm of the leather chair with his cane. It didn't look much, long and thin and whippy, but Toby knew what it would feel like. He turned his eyes away from it deliberately, like he did at the dentist when he saw the drill. He knew what to do. He knelt on the elephant's foot, leant over, gripped the other arm of the chair, closed his eyes, stiffened himself and waited. He heard Rudolph take a deep breath, the cane tapping Toby's trousers. Rudolph was taking aim. Toby's whole body was suffused with a sudden prolonged and searing pain that only began to dissipate when he had stood up again and was rubbing himself, his legs trembling, his mouth full of tears. 'So that you'll never forget, Jenkins, that blasphemy is wicked,' said Rudolph.

'Yes, sir,' Toby managed, and then he realised he had wet himself.

Rudolph walked over to the rolltop-desk and stood the cane in the corner. He turned round and sighed. There was a tremble in his voice. 'I am sorry, Toby, particularly after yesterday, after your recent sad news, but you understand I hadn't any choice. You do understand that, don't you?'

'Yes, sir.'

'Off you go now.'

By second lesson it hurt less. What hurt more were the looks he got in break. It was as if he had some contagious disease. No one came near him, even Hunter seemed absorbed in his own misery and kept his distance. He saw Swann leaning up against a tree crying his eyes out. He felt for him, but he could not bring himself to deal with anyone else's pain.

They were in lunch, just beginning their rice-pudding when the car came for Christopher. Everyone craned to look as Christopher's mother got out and walked across the gravel to the front door where Rudolph and Cruella were waiting for her. They had just finished stacking the bowls when Christopher was seen to walk alone to the car with his suitcase. He looked up once at the building, then at the dining-hall window. Toby couldn't be sure of it because he was some distance away, but Christopher's face seemed suddenly different, open, happy and released. Then he got into the car and Toby could not see him any more.

'Funny looking Jesus,' said Simpson.

'Where's his halo?' said someone else. Major Bagley, substituting for Rudolph at the High Table, sounded the gong and they stood for grace. No one listened to it, not that they ever did. Matron helped Cruella load the trunk into the boot. There was no shaking of hands, only a curt exchange of nods as they stepped back from the car and Christopher's mother got in, slamming the door after her. Major Bagley was still droning through the grace in his dreary monotone. He finished with his customary sing-song flourish.

'*Per Jesum Christum dominum nostrum.*' Hardly anyone said 'Amen'. The wheels skidded in the gravel as the car moved off and vanished up the drive in a cloud of dust and leaves. Christopher was gone. 'Jesus Christ has missed his rice-pudding,' said Simpson under his breath, but to Toby's surprise no one laughed.

There was barbed mockery that afternoon, of course, and Toby was not immune to it. They called him 'Saint Jinks' and he found a cut-out halo on his peg in the changing-room; but the mockery was muted and he could ignore it. Worse to witness was Porter crowing his triumph, his star firmly in the ascendant now. With Christopher discredited and banished, he lost no opportunity in regaining the sway he had held over the school. In just a few hours he managed to take back all the ground he had so publicly lost to Christopher the day before. The war with the oiks, he announced, was on again, the truce was null and void.

So Christopher had been right about Porter too, but

even Porter could not afford to be too spiteful about Hunter and Toby. After any caning there was a natural solidarity amongst the boys. Almost everybody at the school had climbed the Bloody Steps and faced the leather chair. They knew what it was like, what Toby and Hunter must be feeling; and whilst there was little or no positive sympathy, most had the grace to leave them alone. None of the teachers said a word to him except Pricey who told him he'd feel a lot better after a good game of rugby. 'Sorts out most things,' he said. But it didn't.

All through the game that afternoon he tried to hate Wanda for what she'd done, and it wasn't difficult to hate her, not at first. But when he began to think it out he couldn't get it out of his head that she'd done no more than he'd done himself. He'd broken a confidence, he'd broken faith, so had she. She must have told someone, but he still couldn't work out why, or who. He tried not to tackle or be tackled because it hurt him when he fell down.

Hunter, too, played as if he was in a daze, dropping the simplest passes and drifting about the field unconcerned and uninvolved. Pricey finally became irritated. He took them both aside and told them they'd be out of the team if they went on like that. Uncharacteristically Hunter shrugged and walked away, and Toby found that he didn't care any more if he never played for the First Fifteen again.

It was in the changing-room after the game that he first heard that Benedict Swann had gone missing. He hadn't turned up for games and no one could find him. Frantic teachers were out scouring the grounds, and every room, every cupboard was being checked; but by supper-time Swann had still not been found. Word had got about that he had packed a suitcase. There was no doubt now, Swann had run away. A police car was seen coming up the drive and Rudolph left the dining-hall in a hurry. A police sergeant, looking over-heated and anxious with his cap under his arm, addressed the whole school from the High Table, asking everyone if they knew where Swann might be, and if so, that now was the time to speak up. 'Once darkness falls,' he said, 'things could get very difficult for a young lad out there on his own. He's only seven, you know.' From the look on his face he clearly expected some response as he looked around the dining-hall. There was none forthcoming. 'Well, some-one must have seen him,' he said, scanning the hall. 'You mean to tell me that no one even saw him go off?' He gave up after that and left saying that he hoped if anyone remembered anything they'd tell Mr Stagg. Rudolph was wild-eyed with anxiety as he escorted him out.

Toby met up with Hunter that evening after prep. 'I was thinking about Swann,' said Toby, 'all through prep I was thinking. He could be in the chapel down in the park. What do you think?'

'Worth a try, I suppose,' Hunter replied. He seemed preoccupied and distant.

They walked down through the spinney together, a silence between them. Toby wanted to talk but he didn't know where to start. In the end it was Hunter who spoke first.

'You still hurting?' he said.

'When I sit down,' said Toby, and they exchanged a smile of mutual suffering.

A crowd of boys came charging down the hill behind them, Porter and Runcy amongst them. Hunter and Toby stood to one side as they passed.

'Watch out, watch out, there's saints about,' Simpson quipped.

'Idiot,' said Hunter, and lapsed into silence again.

As he crawled into the chapel Toby called out for Swann. If he was in there he didn't want to frighten him, but there was no reply. Toby could see at once that the place was empty. Hunter scuffled through the straw and sat down, leaning back on his hands.

'He's run off after Christopher, hasn't he?' said Toby. 'And we were supposed to look after him.' Hunter picked at a stalk of straw. He wasn't listening. Toby could tell that, but he went on nonetheless. He needed to talk to someone. 'I think he believed in Christopher even more than we did, and he didn't even know who he was, did he? He owned up before we did.' He sat down beside Hunter and went on, feeling braver all the time. 'Now he's not here any more I can tell you. I wasn't sure, you know; I've never been sure, if he was telling the truth, I mean. Sometimes I think he was; then, well . . . for instance, about Jenny, if she's not better then how come he said she would be? And there's another thing I've been thinking about, if he could heal me, why couldn't he heal himself that time? I don't understand . . .'

Hunter sat up suddenly. 'Why didn't you say all this before?' he said. 'Why didn't you tell me? You were always so sure of him. Why didn't you say something? I thought it was just me.' He kicked out angrily at the straw at his feet and hugged his legs, his chin on his knees. 'It was me. I betrayed him. I told someone, about him being Jesus. I told someone.'

'No,' said Toby quite automatically, 'no you didn't.'

'I did, I tell you,' Hunter snapped back. 'I went to see Holy Jo. I had to ask someone, someone who knows about Jesus and things, about God. I had to find out if it could be true. I thought he would help, you know, like a confession. In chapel it was, yesterday evening, and he promised, he promised he wouldn't tell. I told him everything, all about us, about Jenny, everything.'

'What did he say?'

'Same as Rudolph, that it was blasphemy or something. "Wicked," he said, "wicked". And then he just got up and left. He snitched on us, the bastard. He went straight to Rudolph and told him, I know he did. I'm sorry, Toby, I didn't mean it, honest I didn't. And now Christopher's gone and Swann's gone, and . . .' he was crying. Toby had never seen Hunter cry before, he didn't know he could.

'And you've got a sore bum,' said Toby, 'and I've got a sore bum.' Hunter looked at Toby and laughed through his tears. Toby laughed with him out of sheer relief.

Wanda had not betrayed him. She had kept her word. She did love him, she really did. Taken over by their laughter and tears they rolled in the straw until they were too exhausted to laugh or cry any more. They lay there now breathless, looking up at the canopy of rhododendrons.

It was shortly after that they heard a shout go up from the park below. They paid little attention at first. Then there were voices outside. 'Quick, it's Swann!' It sounded like Runcy. 'The oiks have got him. They've kidnapped him. They've bloody kidnapped him!'

By the time Toby and Hunter had scrambled out of the chapel, Runcy, Porter and several others were hurtling down Woody Hill towards the river. Boys were converging on the bank by the fishing-hut from all ends of the park. A pair of wild duck made off protesting down-river. Toby couldn't keep up with Hunter's long legs and was left behind. He stumbled more than once before he reached the bank and pushed his way in beside Hunter to get a better look.

Benjie was standing waist-high in the river, Wanda beside him, holding a suitcase. Benedict Swann lay limp and wet in Benjie's arms.

'I fished him out of the river,' said Benjie wading towards them. 'He's all right, bit off his head though. He said he was running away, looking for Jesus, he said.' Benjie set him down on the bank in front of Toby. 'There y'are, back where you belong,' he said, and Wanda put the suitcase down beside him.

Swann sat there dazed and dripping. 'He says he wants to go home,' said Wanda. Someone's got to say something, Toby thought; and then Hunter spoke up. 'Thanks,' he said.

'You'd better get him back,' said Wanda, 'he'll shiver to death else.'

There was a school match the next Saturday, and they were losing by a single try at half time. Over the oranges Pricey went wild and gave them a royal rollicking. But Toby was happy. Wanda was there on the touch-line watching him, his sweater like a knight's favour wrapped around her shoulders.

In the second half Toby intercepted a pass and ran the length of the pitch to score a try to draw the match. He was still glowing when the final whistle went. Wanda gave him his sweater and told him he was 'brilliant'. He felt it.

As Toby trooped off muddied and exhilarated Matron came over, Swann alongside her, swamped in scarves. 'Showing off fit to bust again, Jenkins,' she said smiling.

'Yes, Matron,' he said. And then he was aware of a hush falling around the ground. Everyone seemed to be looking in one direction, towards Mr Birley's house at the far end of the playing-field. Mr Birley was walking out across the field, Mrs Birley with him, and between them was Jenny, holding their hands, running a few steps and swinging.

'My God!' Matron whispered, 'She's up. She's better. That's the first time that child's been on her feet in a year.'

Swann looked up at Toby and smiled. 'See?' he said.